TAP ROOTS

A Family story of growth
through love, laughter, and
acceptance

Written by
Jane Byrd Lamberson

ISBN: 979-8-9855041-1-8

With supervision from Scotchwood Hill Publishing Service

Cover art by Josh Gunter

Dedication

I want to dedicate this book to all the students whom I was privileged to teach for the thirty- five years of my teaching career at Bay Public Schools in Bay, AR. My very favorite students I was allowed to teach are my four grandsons, Kolby, Kolin, Knox, and Sloan Lamberson. Their love gets me through each day, and I hope their thoughts of Grandma will make them strong everyday of their lives.

Foreword

Many thanks to friends and family who have encouraged me to publish my first book. In 1974 I told my first class of second graders that when I grow up, I want to become an author. To which they replied, "But you are already a grown up!" Many days my friends and family have doubted that fact.

My sisters, Jean Grisham and Laquida Williamson, listened endlessly to my writing ideas and even promised to put this manuscript in my coffin if I failed to get it published. My neighbor and teacher friend, Hilda Wilcox, spent many hours helping me edit. Without her help with grammar and punctuation, my ideas would not be as clear as I intended. Also, my writer friends, Patricia Clark Blake and Martha Rodriguez, helped in getting all my ideas to flow more clearly. Thanks also to a former student, Josh Gunter, for the beautiful art on the cover. It makes me smile

Much love to my two sons, Blake and Brett, who never gave up on my dream to become an author. Every time they asked, "How's the book coming, Mom?" I was more determined to overcome my writer's block. Even Covid-19 played a part in the completion of this book. I could not travel so I wrote.

Finally, the biggest thanks of all to my mom, Joyce Nix Byrd, who taught me by example the joys of reading and writing.

Jane Lamberson 2021

ONE

Apple Core!

Baltimore!

Who's your best friend?

NOT MY FAVORITE GAME, but I do love eating apples. My sister, Fran, always answers that I am her best friend. Then everyone throws their apple cores at the person named as the best friend. Crazy? Maybe, but a good game of chase breaks out. That is what we do for fun in a small, sleepy southern town like Franklin, Mississippi. I remember times when I would name Elvie as my best friend. No, not my boyfriend. Just a friend that happens to be a boy. A boy who often is annoying but also is trustworthy and always painfully honest. Mostly annoying. But, what did an eight-year-old tomboy know about friends? Not much. Granny always said no one can have too many friends. Sure, I have friends, but for the most part, my family keeps my head spinning. Grownups!

On the day I was born, my dad planted an oak tree in the backyard. Does that sound like a lasting memorial from a loving father? Well, the tree lasted, but my father didn't. I refused to call that ole tree a memorial. Popaw and Granny tell me watering the tree is one of my chores, so I sometimes do what I'm told. Granny has wanted me to water it from the time I was old enough to walk. My father left before I could walk. That tree and I are almost eight years old now, and Popaw says we are both growing like a weed. If keeping a tree alive is so important, why all the big mystery about the person who planted the tree?

My mom, June, never mentions his name and quickly leaves the room every time I ask questions. And yes, I do ask a lot of questions. Fran, my big sister, never misses a chance to complain about my questions, how I am dressed, or generally how I act. She is three years older than I am. She has a lot of answers, and I am the one with all the questions that so many adults refuse to answer. I wonder why people act the way they do, and I usually end up with more questions and even fewer answers.

Oh yeah, my name is Ruby—Ruby Ann Kendrick. I feel kinda weird having the last name of someone I've never met. I wish I could have Popaw's name. Ruby Ann Moore sounds like a strong name, and my Popaw and his family have lived in Hilton County for over one hundred years. Popaw says his family always stayed in one place. He also says that his family has strong roots here. Wow! If I stay put and live here as long as the Moore family has lived in Franklin, Mississippi, I will be one hundred and eight. Frank and Alice Moore are my popaw and granny's names. I am stuck with Ruby Kendrick, and nobody wants to talk about how I got stuck with a stranger's name.

"Some people feel the need to roam," says Granny.

"Well," said Popaw, "some people need to learn life isn't easy." Granny never gives him a chance to say much more than this about my dad. When she rolls her eyes and puts her hands on her hips, we all know it is time to change the subject. The last time this happened, I was ready with some exciting news. The county fair would be opening in just about ten days, and I need to do some extra chores to earn some money to ride the Ferris Wheel and the Scrambler as many times as possible.

Mom, Fran, and I live in a big farmhouse with Granny and Popaw. Popaw says making ends meet is how he passes all his time these days. Making a living on a forty-acre farm in Franklin, Mississippi, is not always easy. Momma does laundry for some town people, we raise cotton and soybeans, and we do fine without Ted Kendrick in our lives. That's my dad's name, Ted Kendrick. Just saying his name gives me a funny feeling. There is no face to that name. If that ole tree dies, that will be just fine by me. Now Fran does feel different about that tree, and she even claims it is part hers since the tree Dad planted on her birthday got wiped out when the tornado hit the Franklin area when she was little. When it needs watering or fertilizing from the chicken pen, she claims it is MY tree. Truth be told, it is Granny's tree. Makes no difference to me. We both enjoy being outside--talking or not talking. I just don't like carrying water, but I love being with Granny.

"Ruby Ann, isn't that a wonderful sound?"

"What sound, Granny?"

I don't hear anything except the water sloshing around in the half-full-five-gallon bucket. We are on our way to the far side of the yard where Granny's rose bush and the oak tree stand among twenty million Crepe Myrtle bushes that Granny loves so much. That water is cold on my bare legs. It is even running down into my old tennis shoes, and it's starting to make a squishy sound.

"Just the sounds of no one talking and knowing that things are going to work out, somehow."

"I wish I knew how things are gonna work out at the fair next week."

"Have a little faith, Ruby Ann. I have some change put back from selling eggs. I know you and Francis Jane wanna go to the fair, so be patient and try not to spill any more of the water, okay?"

"How much change have ya got?"

"You will know soon enough, girl, just make sure that you don't leave your bike out of the shed again, and I better not hear you and Fran fussing and calling names like I did last night when you should've been asleep."

"Yes, ma'am. If you enjoy silence, that's what you're gonna get!"

HILTON COUNTY FAIR OPENS SOON!
Friday, August 21   3pm- 10pm.
COME ONE COME ALL!

When I read the sign posted on the telephone pole by Watkins Store, I got so excited that I ran all the way home to tell Granny. She'd been talking about making her prize-winning Bread and Butter pickles for over a week, and yesterday, she picked the best cucumbers from the garden.

"Granny, … Momma…where is everybody?"

"We're sitting on the back porch, shelling peas, and enjoying the quiet until just a few minutes ago," replies Momma with a grin.

"The fair opens next Friday. I am so excited I could just about pop right open."

Granny's eyes sparkle as she says, "Well, come over here and tell me about that spelling test ya took today at school, and then we'll know if there is going to be some more popping on your backside."

"Oh, yeah, it's right here in my pocket, and my teacher says she's right proud of the way my scores have improved. See, it says much improved, with a smiley face right beside the score."

"And is the score 100?"

"Momma, the teacher is proud of my 90%. Only one person made a 100%, and you know who that would be. Elvie Clark.

"Come here, Ruby Ann. I'm proud of you no matter what your spelling score. This 90% is a reason for celebration." Momma reaches into her apron pocket.

She shows me four shiny dimes, waiting for the day that she can reward Fran and me for something special. A 90%

spelling score is special for me since my usual grade is between 60-80. Now, Fran is another story. What would happen if she brought home a 90% spelling paper? Well, you'd think the world might be coming to an end with all the fussing and bawling because her score isn't perfect.

Momma would never fuss, but Miss Fancy Pants Francie would bawl like a baby! Fran's dimes would be awarded when she became the top student in her grade at the end of the term. She is sure to get the top student award, or at least Fran tells us that several times every week this entire school year. There is no way she will spend her money on rides at the fair. Oh, well, that's what makes the world such an interesting place. We are all different. Some more than others, or at least that's what Granny says, and she is the smartest person I know.

The fair opens at 3:30, so I beg Momma to let me go early. Maybe it's a little selfish, but I hate it when all those little kids get to the petting zoo with their parents. I try to get there as the owners open up the cages so the food and water are clean. I love the smell of fresh sawdust, and the sounds coming from the midway are a reminder of better times that are bound to find us before much longer. One year I got there in time to hold a rabbit, as long as I promised not to budge an inch. It was easy not to budge an inch as I ran my fingers across the rabbit's head and between his ears. That gave me a peaceful feeling. I could feel his heartbeat. And his eyes looked so shiny and quiet-like, I could tell he depended on me to stay put and take care of him until his owner returned. Being trusted sure makes me feel good. But this year, everyone in the petting zoo is giving me that "get out of the way, kid" look.

Momma makes me promise that I will be waiting at the front gate at 5:00 when the rest of the family arrives after supper. Now it's only 3:45, so I decide to look at the rides so I can make up my mind early and know exactly where I want to get in line. The smell of Cotton Candy, Corn Dogs, Funnel Cakes, and Candy Apples side-tracks me. Momma is holding all my money, so all I can do is look. The smell of cakes frying up in hot grease was a glorious aroma, but at two dollars apiece, I knew I had to spend my money on something that lasted longer than two minutes.

"Hey kid, this is your lucky day! You got a funnel cake and large soda pop over here with your name on it. What kind of soda do ya want?"

I looked behind me, then left and right, before I decide he is looking right at me.

He doesn't know my name, so I'm sure this is all a big mistake.

"Well, if ya don't want it, don't matter to me," The man at the Funnel cake stand turns his back.

"Who me?"

"Yep, I guess so. You're the only kid in cutoff jeans with a dish-water-colored ponytail coming out of the Petting Zoo. Want it, or not? You're getting Root Beer. Now get over here, so I can get back to the stove."

"Is it free?"

"Already paid for. Some man paid $2.50 and told me to keep an eye on the Petting Zoo."

"Sure, mister. Thanks!"

As I savor each bite of the cake and sip from the soda, never once do I wonder how such good fortune has come my way. I go over to lean against a new John Deere tractor as I enjoy each bite of the sweetest treat I have ever tasted. At first, I say that I'm going to take just a tiny pinch at a time, but my good intentions finally give way to pure greedy pleasure. Momma says too much sugar will give anyone pimples for sure, but at the moment, I refuse to think about my complexion when I'm drifting off to heaven with each mouth full. I wish some of the kids from school would come by so I can wave at them and see the look on their faces when they notice my good fortune. Then a thought hits me like a ton of bricks. I have to meet the family at the front gate.

To avoid too many questions, I pitch the cup of ice in a trashcan, along with the greasy paper plate that is void of any remaining powdered sugar. I run in the direction of the entrance gate. There they are, looking around for me as I run around the back of the Home Demonstration Building.

"What is all over your chin? I hope you didn't start picking up chicken feathers in the Petting Zoo," said Fran.

Thank goodness, Momma and Granny have their hands full of homemade pickles and the aprons they have sewn to enter in competition at the Grandstand. I dust off the evidence of my good fortune and tell Fran to mind her own business. Granny is busy taking out fried bologna sandwiches and jars of water for a quick snack as Mom checks her billfold for the money she and Granny have put back for Fran and me.

"Now, sit over here on the ground, child, and get some nourishment before ya take off," said Granny.

"Do I have to, Mommy? I'm not a bit hungry, and I want to be first in line for the Scramble."

"If Ruby is not a bit hungry, maybe we need to check her for a fever," said Granny with a twinkle in her eye.

"Okay, here is your money. Now use it wisely, and be back at the Grandstand in one hour, so we can decide what time we need to leave," Mommy looks down at her watch.

The next hour goes by so quickly that I don't have a single thought about the mystery man who bought me treats. My two dollars goes fast as I run from ride to ride, spending every last penny. Fran and I listen to gospel singing, see a real magic show, and watch big kids from school trying to ring the bell at the top of a giant pole while Granny and Mommy fill out form after form to qualify for the Home Demonstration competition. When my head hits my pillow at 8:00 that night, I feel like the luckiest kid in Hilton County.

The next morning is Sunday, so there isn't much time to contemplate how many men I know who would decide that I deserve some royal treatment at the fair. Even short of time to get ready for church, Fran's curiosity gets the better of her.

"Where in the world did you get white sugar to eat at the fair? You had it all over your face when we met you at the front gate. Come on, tell the truth."

"That is for me to know and you to find out. Maybe I have been saving money, maybe not."

Preacher Brewer always brags on me in Bible class every time I agree to read aloud a scripture that he thinks deserves our attention. He once said something about a star in my crown, which makes no sense because I don't have a crown. But if I have to choose between a crown with a star and a Funnel cake and large soda, you know the answer. Still, I feel like someone deserves a big thank you. After a while, the thought comes to me that I might as well accept the good fortune.

Soon I realize that nothing seems to go the way I have planned. It seems like God doesn't take note of those scriptures that I have been reading aloud because before we can get our cotton picked, ginned, and the bills paid at the Farmer's Co-op, Popaw has a stroke and has to stay two weeks in a Memphis hospital.

When Preacher Brewer asks me to read aloud in Bible class after that, I just say my throat is scratchy, and I decline. Granny says ya gotta take the good times along with the bad. Well, I know I gotta take them, but keeping my chin up during those long months when Popaw is not himself is a real chore. There is no time to think about the mystery man at the fair because now I have extra chores to do before and after school.

Mommy even starts doing laundry and ironing for Mrs. Clark. She is a real nice lady, but Elvie, her only son, is in my class at school, and he is the one person I know I must avoid if I ever hope to get to heaven. It sure is easier to love your enemies when ya don't have to see them very often.

Mom strikes terror in my heart one Saturday morning after my favorite breakfast of warm pancakes, Maple syrup, and bacon fried just the way I like it.

"Ruby Ann, I need a favor. After you get your room straightened up--that shouldn't take you more than fifteen minutes--take this basket of clean laundry down the road to Mrs. Clark."

"Please, Mom, why can't Fran do that chore? I'll gather the eggs every afternoon next week by myself if you don't make me go to the Clark's. You know Elvie Clark is in my class at school this year, and I just can't take a chance of running into him over there."

"Ruby Ann Kendrick, you better not be acting so high and mighty, like you are ashamed to let anyone know we are working hard to help this family stay on this farm. What would your Popaw say if he heard that you were not doing your share to help out? And for your information, every Saturday morning, Fran goes to pick up the Clark's laundry while you are still in bed. Now, enough said, young lady. Get these clothes to Mrs. Clark and tell her I'll have the rest to her by dark on Sunday."

Elvie Clark is the smartest boy in the fourth grade, and he never passes up a chance to remind everyone about his perfect scores on his report card. He has hair the color of brown moss, green eyes, and a right-nice smile, which usually turns into a smirk when the teacher reads spelling scores aloud. At recess, Elvie brags about how someday he'll be a doctor and own the biggest house in Franklin. When I told him it's bad manners to brag like that, he said he isn't bragging, just telling the facts. I shook my fist right in his face and wanted to whack him right then and there, but the teacher came out on the porch. Granny says it takes a big person to keep her temper under control, and I know exactly what she means anytime Elvie Clark is around.

With a basket of fresh ironing, folded towels, wash rags, and other items I just as soon not mention, I start down the road to the Clark's. If God is listening to my prayers these days, I know a real challenge is coming my way. So — I pray. "Please, God, keep me and my temper away from Elvie if he's at home." Maybe this will be the Saturday he's off at one of his 4-H meetings. When I knock on the door, my heart is beating so fast I almost get dizzy. I hear footsteps coming down the hall toward the door, and I start praying again. Please don't let Elvie come.

"Well, hello to you, Ruby Ann. Elvie will be so sad that he missed seeing one of his classmates. He's off to his 4-H meeting. He's the President this year, and that is a lot of responsibility, you know."

"Here is what my mommy has finished. She will send the rest tomorrow before dark if that's okay with you."

"That is just fine. Now you come back another time and visit with Elvie and stay awhile. Okay?"

"I will have to ask my mommy about that. Gotta go now."

I get back home in ten minutes flat, just in time to help Fran hoe the grass from around the newly planted purple hull peas in the garden. Elvie thinks he's special because his family buys their vegetables from the Piggley Wiggley around the corner from the drugstore. He says his momma can't grow a garden because of her allergies, but I don't believe that for a minute. He brags about canned vegetables tasting better than garden vegetables, but I know that is a big fat lie. There is nothing better than fresh purple hull peas, new potatoes, and ripe red tomatoes that we grow every spring and summer. Popaw says that he feels sorry for anyone having to eat food from a can that's been sealed for who knows how long.

After Popaw comes home from the hospital, life in our house changes a lot. He has to rest more than usual, and my granny worries when he takes off on his long walks to check out the fields. When he decides to sell ten acres of the farm to make a loan payment, I know it won't be long before Momma will need to do more than take in laundry to make ends meet.

I still deliver the clean laundry to the Clarks on Saturday. Fran makes the second delivery on Sunday night. Elvie decides not to be 4-H President after all. He is usually sitting on the front porch every Saturday morning, almost like he is looking for me to come up the road. When he waves, I just look the other way. Anyway, it takes both hands to hold the laundry basket, march up the porch steps, knock on the door, and make a quick exit. At least I try to make a quick exit. Today, he offers me a soda pop, a peppermint stick, and even ice cream on a stick. The offer of ice cream almost makes me give up my resolve to ignore him. This time I lie and tell him I have to get home for chores. But when he starts singing a silly song about "Ruby Red Hen coming up the road again," he breaks the last straw. I forget every lesson I have ever heard about turning the other cheek. First, I am careful to put the clean clothes down on the side of the porch, and I march up to the steps and ask him to repeat those words. He does. What else can I do but issue a challenge?

"You come off that porch, and I will teach you some manners since your mamma certainly never did."

I have to admit I'm shocked when he walks down the steps with a smirk on his face. I grab his collar, and I tackle him to the ground, and down he goes.

"Elvie Clark, don't you ever call me Ruby Red Hen again. Now take it back!"

He takes it back alright and even says, "Uncle" before I loosen my knee from his chest.

I look up to see Mrs. Clark opening the screen door and yelling at that exact moment.

"Elvie, darling, are you okay? And you, Ruby Ann. What in the world has gotten into you, coming around here acting like a wild banshee? If you are going to act this way, don't ever set foot on this property again. Just wait until I talk to your mamma."

What Elvie does next puzzles me so much I don't speak a word.

"No, Mom, I am not hurt. Ruby is showing me a wrestling

move that she learned from our coach at school. She only did it because I begged her to, so it's my fault, not hers."

"Well.... It is just not proper for young people to act this way, right here in the front yard where all the neighbors can see and get the wrong idea. Now get in the house and put on some clean clothes. You have grass stain all over you. And apologize to Ruby Ann for getting her hair all messed up. Dear, I do apologize for Elvie's rude behavior."

"Yes, ma'am. I'm sorry, Ruby. I didn't mean to start any trouble. Really!"

As Elvie and his mother retreat into the house, and I hear their footsteps fade on the newly waxed hardwood floor, I am in shock. What just happened? This may be a real problem. His mamma probably won't be around next time he calls me a name.

TWO

I AM FRAN, Ruby's big sister, and I, too, have a story of a tree. My tree was planted by my dad soon after I was born. Momma told us Dad toted the rusty old shovel over his shoulder as she carried me and the scrawny sapling to just the right spot in Popaw and Granny's yard. He'd rolled a dampened rag around the roots to keep them moist. It was about three feet tall when Dad planted a second tree for my sister. I have heard many stories of those trees before our lives took a big change. The changes started right after my sister Ruby was born. When I was three, I helped carry water to the trees, along with momma or Granny. Daddy took a job working at the cotton gin. Trying to help Popaw on the farm after a day at the gin, he was usually too tired to pay much attention to us or the trees.

Once, when it had not rained for two weeks straight, Daddy announced he wanted to check on the tree, and he let me help. As the cold water splashed over the sides of the little pail, ran down my legs, and into my shoes, I remembered looking up at daddy and thinking he must be six feet tall. Actually, he was of medium build and had dark hair the color of the crows that used to eat the corn out of our garden. His eyes were a deep green, and his laugh—his laugh was glorious. He said we looked like Jack and Jill going up a hill carrying our pails of water. His laugh echoes in my memory now. Little did I know that I would have a new baby sister within the year, and the laughter would stop.

I wish I could understand what happened to change my world so much. What transformed our family from a peaceful, loving home into a solemn, often gloomy place? It wasn't what was said that bothered me the most. It was what was not said. It was the unanswered questions, the uncertainty of our future, and the depression that crippled my mother more each day.

Every chance we could, Daddy would take us on a Saturday afternoon picnic, and for a few minutes, Momma would smile. She seemed to enjoy the times with baby Ruby and me. Daddy would play chase down by the creek and hide behind a tree until I found him. After we finished our fried chicken, tomatoes, and potato cakes, Momma wanted to get the baby to sleep, so I went to look for wildflowers to take home for Granny to put on the table in the kitchen. Daddy planned on getting a little nap in too, but when I returned with the flowers, Mom had folded the quilt, and Momma and Ruby were halfway back to the house. Daddy picked me up and set me on his shoulder. We walked slowly back to Granny and Popaw's house, and I dropped the flowers on the ground and let the wind blow them away. I felt like I was on top of the world, and nothing could happen that my daddy wouldn't fix. Soon events took place that proved me wrong.

The following week a tornado hit our county, and the gin shut down for repairs. Daddy started looking for work and came home later and later each day. As it turned out, there seemed to be more and more things that Daddy couldn't fix. When Daddy didn't come home for three days in a row, I tried to talk to Mamma, but too often, she stayed in her room with the light off. Granny took care of Ruby and me most of the time, and eventually, Granny told us that Daddy had found a new place to live. I'm ashamed to say I let my daddy's tree die. Actually, the tornado uprooted my tree, and I ignored it long enough to let it die. My excuse was I just wanted to stay close to momma. That's what happens when your roots are damaged. It's hard to survive.

How long was my daddy going to ignore us? Fear was a real part of those years, fear that Momma might decide to find a new place to live. Ruby started walking at eleven months. She started talking several months later and hasn't slowed down yet. Ruby kept asking me question after question about her daddy. The other kids in first grade had a daddy. Finally, I said that I didn't know, and I didn't care. I thought she was going to cry, so we both cried together. Our tears helped a little, but Granny's hot sugar cookies right out of the oven helped more than anything.

Momma's voice brings me back from all those memories that are all too vivid.

"Fran, I need you to take these clothes over to Mrs. Clark's for me, please."

"Sure, be right there."

As I walk down the dirt road from our house to the main highway that runs through the middle of Franklin, I imagine where my daddy might be. In history class, I'd heard about Michigan factory workers and wondered if he'd gone to save money for the family. Perhaps he's doing construction work somewhere. Does he ever think of us? Maybe he is working and saving every penny so he can buy a house and surprise Momma. He had not liked moving in with Granny and Popaw, but after the tornado destroyed our house, along with about half of the homes in Franklin, Momma thought it was best. Nine years is a long time to be away. Maybe he has forgotten us completely. Maybe he has other children. My thoughts are interrupted by Elvie Clark's loud shrill voice.

"Well, hey, Fran."

There he sits on the front porch, waiting. I don't know what he's waiting for. I had probably made twenty trips over there, either picking up or delivering laundry, and he was always there. Not once had I seen another boy his age over there. Never had I seen him riding a bike, pitching a ball around, or even digging in the dirt. He is in Ruby's class, and she is always outside doing something. Come to think of it, he asks me about Ruby every time I set foot in his yard.

"Fran, where's Ruby?"

"Oh, you know, she has chores she needs to finish. Is your mom home?"

"She has one of her headaches, and I don't dare open that front door until she opens the front blinds. Just leave the basket here. Maybe she'll let me bring over the money she owes ya later. She has lots of cash in her purse, and she gives me an allowance every week. I can buy us three fudge pops down at Watkins store if ya want."

"Oh, thanks anyway, Elvie. Ruby and I are both allergic to chocolate. See ya. I have to hurry home and help Ruby with the chores."

I know it's time to get out of there before I say something to Elvie that might cause Momma to lose the income we need from doing the Clark's laundry. I whisper a prayer that the lie won't get me into any trouble. I was getting used to lying as my friends asked about daddy being gone for so long. When the truth is so uncertain, what else can I do? I know Daddy will be back before much longer. Not Ruby. She says we might as well get used to the idea that he is gone for good.

THREE

I LEFT MY WIFE and two little girls almost ten years ago. 'Ted Kendrick, you will never amount to a plug nickel.' My dad repeated these words over and over. Guess he was right. Why did I let this happen? I knew I'd have a chance to see the girls when I heard that the Barlett Fair would be in Hilton County, Mississippi. I'd been traveling with the Barlett group for over two years, helping to set up the tents and booths along the midway. I am one of the best workers they have because I refuse to spend every paycheck on alcohol and harder drugs, like most other workers. Working keeps me busy, so I don't have to think about deserting my family.

When I saw Ruby going into the Petting Zoo, I thought my heart would beat out of my chest. All the shame of the past eight years came back like a tornado twisting around in my head. I recognized that dishwater blonde ponytail and those pretty blue eyes because she was the image of her mother. I have the pictures Granny gave me when I went by the hospital to check on Frank when he had his stroke. I keep them in my billfold, but I can't bear to look at them after a while. I bet Fran wouldn't come to the fair until later. She always stayed close to her momma and Granny. I am so ashamed of the way I left without an explanation. I acted the same way as my ole man, who deserted my mom and me when I was only five. I swore I would not be the kind of father that he was, but time has a way of changing good intentions.

My dad was abusive, so my life actually got much better after he left. I wonder what kind of life June and the girls have had since I left. But I send money to my family every month, thanks to Granny. That's more than my ole man did. Who am I kidding? I am no better than he was.

Someday, when I have enough money saved up, I'm going back. If only June had made eye contact with me, said a few words, anything to let me know how she felt, maybe I would've stayed. I know I shouldn't have left, but I convinced myself June would be better without me around. Even when I figured out that this second child couldn't be mine, our marriage could've worked. Too late now. How many times have I played out those scenes in my head? I should have been more determined, made some explanations. I should have stayed. I could hear what the people in town would say:

"You're needed here to help your wife with those little girls."

"June will come around after a few months. Just give her time."

"You're lucky to have June's mom to help, but they need ya at home."

But she shut me out and withdrew from her family and friends, even our church friends. If she could forgive herself, I know I could have forgiven her eventually. All those days that I told my boss I couldn't work overtime, even though we needed the money, I thought being home would make it better. It didn't. Nothing seemed to make it better for June and the girls. Then I tried working more hours until the tornado almost destroyed the cotton gin. Without a job, it seemed like the perfect time to leave. I guess I did what June had done. I shut down since everything around me seemed to be falling apart. Granny was there to help with the girls. Seems my father-in-law was right after all. June told me once when we were dating that he said time would tell if that boy would be any different from his old man.

When June started walking to the small bookstore next to Holt's Drugstore, I thought getting out with Fran would be good for her. She always loved to read, and I was too busy to see what was going on right under my nose. Fran was just starting to notice pictures in the few books that we had at the house. She could scribble the first letter in her name. She was so quick to catch on to the nursery rhymes, and she could even carry on a conversation at age two. She sure didn't get that kind of brain from me. When that bookstore opened in Franklin and announced people could borrow and buy books, the business was a hit.

Bradley McDole, the owner, was new to our area. One thing for sure, he had money. No one knew much about him, but he drove the shiniest sports car, the only sports car in our town.

Granny said, "When that young man realizes how little there is to do around Franklin, he won't be here long."

She was right about that. When did this young man from Memphis start to notice June's beautiful eyes and her petite frame? He put soft cloth books on the circle rug in the back of the store for Fran to enjoy. Books that she certainly wouldn't be able to enjoy at home. June said that was so thoughtful. He didn't care about Fran, that's for sure. McDole always seemed to have read the same books that June was reading, so the conversations about those books seemed innocent enough. At least, at first. The books that she got from Bradley's bookstore were all June seemed interested in that spring.

That was almost ten years ago. I am not sure why I have spent ten years wondering and waiting. One thing I needed was the courage to return and admit I was wrong for leaving. I'd thought of hunting down Bradley McDole to make him pay for taking advantage of June. But with no money and the guilt I felt, it was easy to push those thoughts out of my head. June and her parents had nothing but love for the child. I knew I could accept her as my own if June would have me back.

Yet, here I sit at the Franklin County Fair, selling tickets to kids the same age as my two girls. I am less than five miles from a home that needs me. I'm not sure how June's dad feels about me, but Granny has kept her word about the money I send every month. She said it would be our secret as long as Ruby never found out about her real father. Did June even listen when I told her I would love the new baby just like my own? She was a part of our family. June wouldn't agree to get help for her depression. She had a blank look on her face and never spoke a word for months. Then I did what I begged June not to do. I withdrew from the family that needed me. I put miles and miles between us, thinking it would get better. It didn't.

When I saw Ruby going into the Petting Zoo, I knew something had to change. I am nervous about the next big change coming. Listening to the radio at night, I keep hearing about Uncle Sam needing people to enlist for a career in the Army. The bonus would go a long way in helping on the upkeep of Frank and Joyce's farmhouse. Frank's health is not good. If he can't work, that will cause a struggle for four females. I am going down to the recruiting center on my next day off. I have no idea about this place called Vietnam, but I am about to find out. My enlistment will put many miles between me and a difficult situation that I created. Will the guilt go away? Probably not, but my thoughts will be on just staying alive to come back to a family that needs me.

FOUR

I HAVE TWO beautiful daughters that need the attention of their mother. I can see now how selfish I have been. Thank God my momma has been here to fill the gap.

My daddy would say, "June, put those books down, let's go catch us some fish."

My actions caused me to lose a husband who loved me. Why did I get lost in self-pity? Why could I not see the evil in Bradley? Every time I visited the library, he spent most of his time talking to me. He was attentive to Fran and his stories were of places I only hoped to see. How could I have been so wrong about his motives?

The sky was a dull grey that afternoon in November when I started walking to the bookstore to return my borrowed books. After realizing Ted was working late again at the gin, I couldn't bear being in that house another minute. Fran was asleep, and Granny was there to watch her anyway. After I bundled up my sweater and the bags of books to return, I felt excited to just get away for a while. The walk to the store and back would take less than an hour if I hurried. I arrived just as Bradley was putting the cashbox in the small security safe in the backroom. He had decided to close early because there was a chance of snow in the late afternoon.

I have always been such a trusting person. Some people called me naïve. I should never have accepted his offer to give me a ride home. I had never seen a Camaro before. Sure, I would like a ride in one. The sky did look a lot like snow. When he did not turn toward my house, I noticed a look on his face that gave me a chill.

"Please stop the car. I will walk from here."

"Why would you do that? I want to show you where I live. It's not that far out of town. This is a perfect time since you didn't bring your daughter today."

"Bradley, I have a husband at home. No, I don't want to see where you live. I just want to get back home."

"From what I hear, your husband works all the time. Don't you want to have a little fun sometime?"

"Bradley, please don't do this...."

I should have tried to get out of the car but when he sped up so fast, I just froze. When he turned down a deserted road and the darkness was all around, I felt a fear that caused me to shake uncontrollably. As the engine shut off, Bradley scooted closer on my side of the car. I screamed. The rest is a blur and remains a blur to this day.

When the bookstore closed suddenly and Bradley McDole left town, no one was shocked. I was numb, relieved, and angry. Mostly I felt ashamed of myself for not fighting harder. I was relieved that he left town and that my mom never told my dad about the details of Ruby's birth. The town's people said that he was nothing but a spoiled rich kid anyway. There was no way he ever planned to put down roots in a small town like Franklin. After all, he lived in Franklin for over a year, and never once did he come to church. Whoever heard of a bookstore in a town this small? There is no way he could make enough money to keep that store running.

But he left me with his child and a shame that pushed me over the edge. When I fell, a dark place of depression enveloped me. No one in my family could understand, even me.

FIVE

I AM ALICE SMITH Moore, but the most favorite title I wear now is Granny. I am mother to June Kendrick, and her two daughters are the light of my world. Frank, my husband of fifty-five years, is a patient and kind man. He has worked hard all his life to provide for his family. He found the hardest task of all was helping his own daughter out of her depression.

What in the world can I do to help my daughter come to her senses? Frank and I are getting older, and she often seems like more of a child than Frances Jane. She wants to be a good mother, and June is a good mother now. But after Ruby Ann was born and Ted left, I was afraid she would never get over the shame she felt. When Dr. James suggested that we check her into a mental hospital for treatment, I thought Frank would lose all control. He refused to listen to another word the doctor had to say. Mental Illness was a red flag to him. What would he do if he knew June had gotten herself pregnant by that bookstore guy? I don't even want to think about what he would've done.

Frank is a good man but often so full of pride that he won't face the facts. I'm not sure it was the best thing to do, but I kept my letters to Ted a secret. I did promise Ted I would keep him informed about June and the girls. He started sending money along the way that has come in handy.

Secrets have a way of mounting up, one on another, and the years have passed quickly. I would tuck away the money he sent, then write a few lines to let him know that things were getting along okay. We had done well until Frank had that stroke. June seems to be getting stronger since her daddy had to slow down and admit that he can't work long hours on the farm like before. Soon, I must find the courage to tell my daughter that Ted wants to come back. He says he does. There is a fine line between doing the right thing and just talking about the right thing. Only time will tell about Ted and all the secrets that keep sticking up their ugly heads around this family. How can I tell Ruby Ann about her birth father? It isn't my place to do that. It has got to be her mother's place when the time is right. And Fran—sometimes I worry that she is too much like her mother. Maybe June is too much like me. She refuses to face the truth about events that have affected our family. Oh, well, I know I have made plenty of mistakes in my time, and Frank never gave up on me. Frank always says our roots run deep. We can't let bad winds get us down.

We have had our share of bad winds and trials of this life, but we worked through them together. I can understand Frank's reluctance to turn to the medical field for help. Just three years after we were married, Frank's sister took an overdose of a prescription medicine that caused her to become disabled. Frank and his entire family tried to blame the doctor. My sister-in-law could never face the rest of the family when her husband deserted her and her depression spiraled downward. Frank's brothers, the entire Moore family, bottled up their anger for years. My prayer for Frank is that his anger over losing his only sister will not consume his life.

When June was born, Frank was so proud of his only daughter. I could see his love for her start to break down his anger. Earlier, his own brother was sentenced to five years in prison for his anger toward a black man. That is a branch in the Moore Family tree that no one was proud to acknowledge. I think that was a turning point for Frank. He could see the end result of prejudice toward others with a different skin color and his brother's family suffered.

Frank let his anger flair again when June started dating Ted Kendrick. Ted's father was lazy, and this did not fit the ideal husband Frank had in mind for his only daughter. When I reminded Frank that my parents weren't exactly happy when I announced I was going to marry into the Moore family, he thought a long time before he replied.

"I am nothing like my hot-headed brother who let his temper get the best of him!"

"You're right, Frank, and Ted is not the same person that his father proved to be by deserting his family. There's got to be some good in Ted for June to love him as she does. We need to support June in her decision to date Ted."

"Okay, Alice, I see your point. If Ted is a hard worker and proves himself dependable, I'll try to support June's choices."

What proved the hardest for Frank was his inability to help June get over her depression. I am determined to do everything in my power to keep our branch of the Moore Family tree strong.

SIX

WELL, I AM BACK telling the rest of the Kendrick family story. Ruby Ann, sister to know-it-all Fran, daughter of June and Ted, and granddaughter to the best Granny and Popaw in the world. I like to think of myself as Ruby Ann, the one member of my family who is determined to unravel some secrets that have been buried too long.

How did the three of us ever get up the courage to board a bus to Austin? Yes, I will take the credit from the beginning. I still can't believe that Fran and Elvie want to tag along. The idea all began in history class. Each student had to report on a country and do a map display. Mr. Haley, the youngest teacher in the Franklin Elementary School, has a way of making school less boring. Momma thinks he might be a Hippie, whatever that means. He's to blame, I guess, but in a good way because he encourages us to think for ourselves. He always welcomes questions and never makes anyone feel dumb, even if the question seems dumb. We even get to work in groups sometimes, and he doesn't worry about us copying from each other. Weird! He calls the report a current event. He often starts history class by reading an article from the newspaper. We have learned about China, Japan, Italy, but lately he is talking about Vietnam.

We have many questions about Vietnam. When we started, only Elvie Clark knew the country had been split into the northern and southern parts. He has a television, and he never misses a chance to let us all know about world events. But I get interested when Mr. Haley says there is a conflict and many soldiers from the United States are over there.

"Mr. Haley, is it a big war?" I asked.

"It ain't no war. It's a conflict. That's what they call it on the news." Elvie loves any opportunity to embarrass me.

Anyway, Mr. Haley asks us to pick a partner and work together. Elvie picks me and we get Vietnam. I decide a partner with a television set might be a good idea. I won't have to spend so much time looking up stuff in the library. Little do I know that this current event report will end up with Elvie, Fran, and me making our first bus trip without a parental permission form.

We start our notetaking in the school library, and I have never in my life seen anybody more excited about going to the library than Elvie Clark. As long as he sits across the table and not beside me, I agree to meet him after school to begin the report. He agrees to work on the map while I write down facts about the history and why United States troops are being sent to Vietnam. I soon become familiar with cities called De Nang, Hanoi, Hai Phong, and even Ho Chi Minh City.

I mention to Mom and Granny about the things I am learning. Granny tells us that many of our soldiers are in Vietnam because they have been drafted. When she says drafted means that men don't volunteer to fight, I want to learn even more. I thought soldiers always volunteered to fight. And it doesn't seem right to me that only men can be soldiers. I know I can fight better than almost every boy in the fifth grade, and I don't have to try hard. But when I think of Fran being a soldier, well, that doesn't make a bit of sense either. She is more like Momma, quiet and soft inside.

After working two days after school on our Vietnam report, I tell Elvie we better get started on the map part because the whole thing is due in two more weeks. I plan to tape four sheets of paper together to make a big map, but Elvie says his momma has already bought a poster board. What a waste of money.

"Twenty cents! That's crazy." When I think of what I can buy for twenty cents, my mouth waters. Our big map of Vietnam will look great, but I am not about to say that to Elvie. His head is big enough without me letting him know that the poster board is a good idea.

The day before we have to turn in our projects, Elvie comes to my house. Of course, I want to read the report aloud, so Momma and Granny can see how much I have learned about Vietnam. Granny makes sugar cookies, and Momma makes Kool-Aid. Even Fran says she is impressed. We'd have a party, except Popaw doesn't feel like getting out of bed. We take it to his room to show him the poster board map, and he smiles. After a while, I worry that Elvie is never going home, but finally, he leaves. Everything goes back to normal, or almost normal, anyway.

That night, Popaw starts coughing so badly that Momma and Granny decide he needs to see the doctor in the Emergency Room in Austin, forty miles from Franklin. Fran and I have to spend the rest of the night in our nightgowns on Mrs. Clark's couch, no less.

We lay awake for a long time. Trying to rest in a strange place is hard enough, but worrying about Popaw makes it almost impossible. Too many "what ifs" float around in my brain. Fran doesn't want to listen to any of them.

"There is nothing we can do, so please, Ruby, hush."

"But what if the doctor wants to keep Popaw in the hospital? We can't just stay here at the Clarks. What if Elvie gets up early in the morning and sees us in our gowns?"

"Ruby, it's almost midnight. Please hush and quit talking."

"But what if Popaw can't get well and gets so sick that…."

"It's gonna be what is meant to be. Not another word, okay?"

Momma wakes us up early the next morning while it's still dark. After fumbling around quietly to slip on shorts and a t-shirt, I hear bacon sizzling and see light in the kitchen. Mrs. Clark comes to the doorway and convinces my momma to sit down at the kitchen table for fried eggs, bacon, buttery toast, and jelly. Mrs. Clark's store-bought jelly is almost as good as Granny's homemade muscadine jelly. Almost, but not quite. Momma plans to drop Granny and Popaw off at home and go to the drugstore to get some new medicine. I am glad we have to hurry, so maybe I won't have to say anything to Elvie. Just as Fran and I finish stacking the dishes in the kitchen, I hear feet shuffling, and there he is.

"I smell bacon cooking, Mom, and I am so...," Elvie says. "Why do we have company for breakfast? Should I get dressed or stay in these pajamas? Maybe we can play some board games after breakfast. Ya wanna play, Ruby Ann?"

I don't speak a word. Actually, I can't take my eyes off the picture of Howdy Doody on the front of Elvie's pajama shirt and his hair tumbling all over the place. That sight will stay in my mind for a while. Thankfully, Mom tells Mrs. Clark we have to pick up some medicine. We gather up our stuff and make a quick exit.

After a stop at Holt's Drugstore, Mom, Fran, and I head down Highway 555 to our house. When we turn off the highway to go down our lane, Mom suddenly hits the brakes and starts to back up. She stops at the mailbox.

"Ruby Ann, Granny didn't check the mail yesterday because she wouldn't leave Popaw that long. Hop out and get it, please, and don't drop anything. You can walk on up to the house, okay?"

"Are you sure Granny won't get mad, Mom? She tells me she needs the exercise and makes me promise never to touch the mail."

"Just this once, Ruby, it will be fine. Now hurry up but promise to walk slow."

After collecting two catalogs, the electric bill, Popaw's veteran's newsletter, and a small white envelope addressed to Joyce Moore, I hug that stack of mail tightly to my belly until the white envelope slips loose. As I bend down to dust off the envelope, I notice several markings. I am shocked by the return address.

Co. E 1/46 196th LIB

APO San Francisco, California 96374

I find no name, and the bunch of numbers means nothing to me. I know a little bit about San Francisco, California, but the APO makes no sense at all. Who in California would be sending Granny a handwritten letter? I turn it over and even hold it up to the sunlight to see if I could tell what was inside. No luck. I plan to solve this mystery.

Monday drags by at school. I have memorized the return address. I know that Mr. Haley will help me find out exactly what I want to know, and he won't ask a million questions. He always stays after school to grade homework, and I find him in his room with his feet propped up on the desk and a handful of papers in his lap.

"Well, hello, Ruby Ann. Come on in. I really need a break from grading these papers. This isn't my favorite part of being a teacher. What can I help you with?"

"I have a question I hope you can answer for me. I found an old letter right next to the trash can at the post office window in Watkins Store, and I thought maybe you could tell me what all these numbers and letters mean on the return address. I copied down the return address cause it looked weird to me. Here's what it says. I gave it to Mrs. George at the post office, but I want to know what APO means and these other numbers, too."

"Well, it seems you found a letter written by someone in the military. APO stands for Army Post Office and Co. E probably means Company E, but that is just a guess. And that number after APO stands for the country overseas where that person is stationed. Ruby Ann, you need to know that messing with the US mail is against the law. Did you know who the letter is addressed to?"

"No, I haven't ever heard of the name. I can't even pronounce it, but I promise I already returned the letter. Thanks, Mr. Haley. See ya tomorrow in class. Oh, one more question. How can I find out what country the letter came from?"

"A guess would be the public library. Since Franklin doesn't have a library, you will have to get your mom to drive you to Austin to find that information. This is important, Ruby Ann. I don't want one of my favorite students to end up in jail. Don't mess with someone's mail."

"Okay, I promise! Elvie tells me the same thing. Is it true?"

"Sure is, Elvie knows what he is talking about, sometimes."

And then he laughs, and I do too. That is another reason I like Mr. Haley. He enjoys a good laugh.

I have to find a way to get to the Austin Public Library to solve this mystery. Who does Granny know that's in the military? Why will Granny not mention she knows a soldier, even if that person is not in the war? It occurs to me that many people have been in the military who never fought in a war. Whoever is writing to Granny might not be a soldier. Someone has to cook meals, fix vehicles, and even answer the phones. Being in the military can involve many jobs.

My first step will be to find a person who knows my Granny. A trip is in my future, but the details are still very foggy. I could just ask Granny, but somehow, I know she has reasons for not mentioning the letter. Maybe I can ask Momma. No, I need to get to the Austin Public Library. But how?

SEVEN

FRAN KNOWS ABOUT LIBRARIES. When I tell her I need information to find the Austin Public Library, she's thrilled to tell me about a reference book listing all the libraries in the state. She also knows about APO addresses. I make her promise not to tell anyone about the letter I discovered in the mail. She also reminds me there's no way in the world Momma will take us to Austin, especially to answer a question when we can't even tell her the reason. I have another detail to work out. Fran said her class is going to the library on the following Friday, so I have a whole week to make a plan to solve the mystery of the person who writes Granny.

On Thursday morning, Mom and Granny always go to Watkins Store to buy flour, butter, and sugar. They also sell eggs, if we have extra. In two weeks, school will be out for the summer, so a plan begins to form in my head. I know Thursday will be a good day to go, but getting to Austin, more than thirty miles away, will be the real challenge.

One day during recess, Elvie mentions that he and his mom had taken the bus to Austin to visit a museum about famous people from Mississippi. I wonder how much that cost. I am sure that there is a bus schedule somewhere at the post office. As much as I hate to admit it, Elvie Clark has some answers to many of the questions I have. Before I can get any closer to finding out more about the mystery letter, I have to get to Austin. I'm going to the Austin Public Library on a bus on the first Thursday after school is out. I'm going to find out more about APO number 96374. Then with all the courage I can muster, I plan to have several serious talks.

My first serious talk will be with Elvie because he has a phone. If he is to be believed, he has enough money to take a bus trip. I ask Elvie to meet me in the school library at 3:30.

"Why?" Elvie asks.

"Why? I need your help. I kinda thought you might want to help me solve a mystery."

Again, he says one word, "Why?"

I reply, "Why not?"

"Ruby Ann Kendrick, why would you ask me for help when most of the time you make faces at me if I try to talk to you? About a month ago, you pinned me down and made me say uncle, all because I tried to talk to ya."

"Well, I am ashamed of myself for all that wrestling stuff, and I promise that won't happen again."

"Okay, then, forget about it. What do you want my help with anyway?"

"I need to get to the Austin Public Library to find out about a military address on a letter that came to my house. Can you help me or not?"

"Well, I guess I might if you know the APO address."

"Elvie, how do you know about an APO address anyway?"

"That is for me to know and you to find out, Miss High and Mighty!"

"Elvie Clark, you quit all that name-calling, or I am going to break that promise I just made about wrestling you down."

"Sorry, Ruby. I am just not used to anyone asking for my help, but I do want to help you find out whatever it is ya want to know about that address. I do have one condition."

"And what would that one condition be?"

"You gotta let me go on that bus trip to Austin with you, and I will not let another person know about it, cross my heart and hope to die. Deal?" Elvie flashes his wicked smirk.

"Deal. When can we start getting our bus trip planned?"

"Well, slow down, Ruby. How do you plan on sneaking away long enough for the three-hour trip to the Austin Public Library?"

"It will take a pack of lying, but I know I can work out the details if you can get our tickets. Fran has agreed to find the address."

"The money is no big problem for me. After my daddy left, he set up a trust fund and...."

"Please spare me the details. Can ya get the tickets or not?"

"Sure!"

"Elvie, remember not another soul can know about this. Do you really mean it? Cross your heart and hope to die, stick a thousand needles in your eye?"

"You bet I mean it. This is gonna be fun!"

"You've got to be kidding me, Ruby. Elvie Clark is not going to buy you a bus ticket anywhere. His mother will never allow him out of her sight."

"I know I can work out all the details. Fran, that's why I needed the address out of the reference book."

"Please, Ruby, if you are so set on getting information about the mystery letter, just ask Granny. Stop all this wild talk about sneaking off to the Austin Public Library."

"No way am I backing out now. The bus leaves from Holt's Drug store at 8 AM. Elvie says the round trip will take about three hours. We can get the information from the library in maybe 30 minutes or so. We can be back home by 12:30 or maybe an hour later."

"Sounds like a lot of maybes to me," said Fran.

"Well, maybe you should go along with Elvie and me, so if momma finds out, we will be grounded together. What do you say, Fran, wanna go along to protect your little sister and Elvie?"

"No! I won't have anything to do with all this lyin'. And you will get caught. There is no doubt in my mind."

"I believe you already have a part in the plan because you did give me the address of the Austin Public Library."

"Yeah, well, Momma doesn't know that. Please promise you won't tell Momma. Please, Ruby. I only want to help you solve your mystery. I never dreamed you would take it this far."

"That seems like one of your real problems. You never dream — period."

When I see the look in Fran's eyes, I know I hurt her feelings. She turns and runs behind the house. I decide to follow her to try to take some of the bite out of my hurtful words. I know I need Fran on my side, so as hard as it is for me to apologize, it has to be done. The only thing I can l think about is the excitement of taking a bus trip and solving the mystery of Granny's letter. Maybe the letter is from an uncle I have never met. Maybe Granny has another family that she keeps secret. Did Popaw know anything about a secret admirer?

I find Fran sitting under the oak tree in the backyard. She holds her head in her hands, and her shoulders shake slightly. I know not to talk for a while, so I sit down beside her and think about my next words. Granny's words echo in my mind. "Ruby Ann, you must think before you speak. Words can really hurt sometimes. Once they are out, you can't take them back."

"Fran, I didn't mean what I said about you not having any dreams. Everyone knows I am the one in this family with the problems. My big mouth is always getting me into trouble. I just want to make some sense of Granny's letters. Forget what I said about your part with the address. I won't tell Mommy. I promise. But you have to promise me not to tell anyone what Elvie and I have planned. Okay?"

As Fran lifts her head and wipes her eyes and cheeks on

her T-shirt, she starts to laugh. She laughs so hard that I think she will start crying again. I wonder if she thinks our plan is that crazy or if she truly enjoys hearing me apologize.

"You are right. You do have a big mouth. But I do have dreams that you know nothing about. Now, I have decided that two ten-year-old kids can't board a bus, unchaperoned, without having a few questions asked. If Elvie can manage three bus tickets, I will go along on this mystery-solving trip and hope that all your maybes can work out just as you have planned."

For once, I can't think of a single reply. It's a miracle, plain and true. Now I know that I might as well start praying for another miracle because in two and a half weeks, I will be taking my first bus trip ever. Elvie Clark and Fran going along seemed like a dream. Hopefully, this trip won't turn into a nightmare.

EIGHT

THE FOLLOWING TWO WEEKS at school seem to drag. The teachers are just as glad to be getting off for the summer as the kids are. We don't have much homework either. The teachers tell us to bring a book to read because they'll make no assignments as long as we're quiet. Every afternoon as I walk home, Elvie falls in beside me and asks a million questions about the trip. Will we need a snack on the bus? How far is the library from the bus station? What is the next step after we find what country is represented by the APO address? His questions keep coming until I almost regret asking him to help me. But it will take me years to save up enough money for bus tickets. Elvie says tickets are the least of his worries. He has to work out an alibi about his absence from eight in the morning until the afternoon that will sound logical to his mom. She knows he doesn't have many invitations to spend time with his friends. Oh, well, that is his headache, not mine. But, if he gets caught in a lie, Fran and I will also be discovered missing. As much as I hate to admit it, we need to get our stories together.

There is little time to be alone with Fran and Elvie on Sunday to plan our getaway to Austin. After breakfast, Fran and I dress in our best clothes, which are not comfortable, to say the least. I know God knows and sees everything that goes on in this world, but why would it matter to Him if I show up for church in jeans and a t-shirt? No one ever mentions Sunday shoes at our house, but I notice Elvie and a few others have shiny shoes they wear only once a week. Talk about wasting money. Shoes won't wear out for years if the soles only hit the ground for two hours a week. Tennis shoes scrubbed hard on Saturday night suit me just fine. I know they please God, too.

Elvie passes me a note after Bible class. He will be at my house at 3:30 that afternoon to TALK. He also says to get a fishing pole ready. Any other time I would have flat out said no, but if we're boarding a bus in two weeks, we have details to work out. I pray a lot that Sunday, mainly that we will be able to sneak out and get back home safe. In the back of my mind, I keep thinking that honesty is the best policy. But I know that getting to Austin and back will take a heap of lying.

You gotta love Jesse Adams. He is in the same grade as Elvie and me. He has nothing in common with Elvie, but he is pretty easy to get along with most of the time. Now, his older brothers are bad news. They make weekly visits to see the principal.

Jesse will do anything for money. Well, maybe not anything, but he sure is willing to help Elvie with a few lies to Mrs. Clark and a string of catfish from Mr. Sutton's pond. We are getting closer to our joint alibi. The Adams family has ten kids, a small farm, and a mean hound dog that scares away all unwanted visitors, especially Elvie. I know he is determined to go on our bus trip when he suggests Fran and I walk over to Jesse's house that Sunday afternoon. Momma says as long as we are back before dark, we can walk to Sutton's Pond. We don't mention stopping by Jesse Adam's house. That information will stir up more trouble and make us tell more lies later on down the road.

Elvie told Jesse at school that he needed a favor, and he would pay two dollars if Jesse would help provide an alibi for the morning of May 21. I will never forget how nervous Elvie and I were as we approached the front porch of Jesse's house. Sutton's Pond lay on the forty acres behind their house, and the Adams kids fish there anytime as long as they report to Mr. Sutton if anyone else shows up. Jesse is waiting for us with his hand on Buford's collar. Buford is a brownish-colored bloodhound that looks harmless until he bares his teeth. No growl--no lunging forward--just teeth that are yellow, sharp, and plentiful. When Buford snarls, Elvie screams and jumps behind me like his life is in danger.

"Don't mind Buford. He always does that with his teeth, if he doesn't know ya," said Jesse. "Do you have the two dollars or not?"

With all the courage he can muster, Elvie replies, "Sure, but first, can you just put Buford under the porch, so we can talk about what you gotta do before you get both dollars? I will give you one dollar today. Then when we agree on the fish, you can come to my house on Thursday and get the rest. Okay?"

"Sure. I'll come over on Wednesday afternoon and act like we're big buddies. I'll tell your mom that if you can meet me at Sutton's Pond at 5:30 on Thursday morning, then I know we can have a string of fish by four that afternoon. Now, when will I get my other dollar?"

"Ruby and I will come to your house about 3:00. After I show her the fish, you can take those smelly things back with ya."

"Ya mean I can keep the fish and two dollars? Wow! This is the best deal I have ever made. Thanks."

"No way do I want those smelly, slimy fish at my house. You will get your other dollar after we show Mom the fish. Deal?"

"Deal. Easiest money I've ever made in my life."

As we walk away, I tell Elvie that he did a good job with his alibi. He must still be nervous about Buford because he never says a word. After walking almost to my front porch, he finally speaks to me.

"Thanks for letting me go along with you and Fran. I think you're the bravest person I have ever met, Ruby. Sure hope this trip helps you find out more information about the mystery letter. Do ya think the person writing your Granny is your dad?"

I couldn't be more surprised if lightning struck me at that very minute.

"Elvie Clark, what in the world makes you think that? You are crazier than you look, and if you ever mention my daddy again, you'll wish you were dead. Now, get out of my sight before I lose my temper."

"Gee, Ruby. I don't mean anything about your dad. It's just I don't know anything about my dad, and I am too scared to ask, that's for sure. Forget I said anything. I'm leaving now."

NINE

MAY 21 FINALLY ARRIVES. Fran and I didn't get much sleep the night before our first bus trip. Granny and Mom leave to sell eggs, tomatoes, and homemade pickles at the Farmers' Market. Popaw is eating his breakfast in his room as Fran, and I put the dishes away. We give him a hug and kiss and tell him we're off to fish at Sutton's Pond and will see him for a late lunch. He comments that he's glad Fran and I are spending the morning together. A twinge of guilt puts a knot in my stomach.

Elvie has assured us that he has our tickets, and his mother will be over at his Aunt Sally's house all morning playing Bridge since she thinks Elvie is fishing with his new buddy, Jessie. Unless the bus has problems, we will be rolling into Austin by 9:30 and return to Franklin by 1:00. Can this really happen the way we have planned? Too late to back out now.

When Fran and I get to Holt's Drugstore at 7:55, Elvie is waiting for us, dressed in his Sunday best suit, shiny shoes, and a tie. I could have died right there. His smile is so big that I decide not to mention how out of place he looks with his fancy clothes. Maybe Fran and I are the ones not dressed for the occasion, but none of that seems to matter now. Eight other people are waiting inside the store for the bus, and not a single person looks like they are heading to a Sunday meeting. Elvie doesn't let that bother him. He shows every ounce of nerve he owns just lying to his mom about the day's activities.

"I've got a change of clothes for when we get back this afternoon. My mom has already told the entire Bridge club about the fish we are sure to catch. Oh, and I brought some snacks in case we get hungry, wet wipes for our hands, paper and pencil, and …."

"Elvie, please tell me you have our bus tickets," Fran says in her most polite voice. I am glad she stops Elvie from talking because what I want to say is not polite at all.

"Oh, yes. I have them right here in my sock. I put all three tickets there last night and even slept in my socks so I wouldn't forget them. I am so excited about…. "

"We can tell how excited you are, now please hush. Everyone is gonna be staring at us," I say.

As the bus comes slowly around the curve from the school, I grab Fran's hand and leave Elvie standing there holding his brown bag of goodies.

"I think we should be the last ones on the bus. In case there are any questions, we can make a quick exit," I tell her.

"Good idea," said Fran. "Come on, Elvie. Stand over here with us, and forevermore, get the tickets out of your sock without being seen."

I notice an older couple from church coming out the door

of Watkins' Grocery. Most Sundays, Mr. and Mrs. Turner sit three pews behind us and always nod to Granny and Popaw when we leave. Maybe they won't recognize Fran and me. No such luck. They walk right over to Fran and ask how Popaw is feeling these days. In her most grown-up voice, she tells them he gets stronger every day. The three of us head toward the bus, but Mrs. Turner isn't finished. She directs her next question to Elvie.

"Well, look at you, Elvie. You're all dressed up and in the company of these two lovely young ladies. How did you get so lucky to take a bus trip without your momma?"

"Well — we are making a trip for a special school project. You know Momma wants me to be the top student in our grade, and Ruby and I are doing research hoping for an A+. We are doing some research on the history of the Austin Public Library."

When he mentions my name, Elvie reaches over and grabs my hand like he expected me to say something. No way is that going to happen, so I take a few steps toward the oncoming bus. Elvie hangs on tight, and I drag him along as far from the Turners as we can go. I bump into a young mother holding the hand of her two-year-old. The little boy sticks out his tongue at me, and I do the same to him. I'm not sure why I do that, but standing there holding Elvie's hand is just too weird. I glance back to see Fran talking to the Turners, so I drop his hand. I start to stick out my tongue at him but change my mind.

As the bus stops, the door opens. I say a silent prayer that this day will pass quickly, and no one discovers this wild scheme I dreamed up. It all seems like a dream until I hear the driver's booming voice.

"You kids need to back up. Ya can't board without an adult. Step back."

For once, Elvie and I don't know what to say, so we step back just as he told us. As the Turners board and two other people get on, Fran steps up to take control.

"These two young people are in my charge today. I'm sixteen years old, and I have a letter with written permission from their parents. I'm a Junior on the Honor Roll at Franklin High School. I'll be glad to show you the letter."

"Okay, little lady, I have a schedule to keep here, and I'm not much on reading. Show me three tickets, and we can be on our way."

He inspects the tickets and deposits them, and we start down the aisle. I go all the way to the back seat. Only one other person is sitting in the last two rows, so I know we have plenty of room, but Elvie grabs my shoulder to stop me from sitting there. I'm just about to lose my temper when I hear the bus driver's gruff voice again.

"Okay, Miss Honor Roll, you surely know that only Blacks can sit on the last two seats. Get seated in the right spot if you are going to be in charge. Now."

Every eye on the bus seems to be glued on us as Fran leads us to the nearest empty seat. She sits down first, and I nod for Elvie to sit by her. I want some peace on my first bus trip ever. One thing for sure, I've got many questions about those last two seats. We don't have any Blacks in our whole school, but I know several Black families that live right outside the Franklin city limits. Those kids have to go to school somewhere, right? Oh well, I will be sure to talk to Mr. Haley about this when school starts back in the Fall.

We pass Franklin Elementary School and several tiny houses that look like the house where we live. They have white siding and a porch that runs the entire length of the house. The scene makes me think about Popaw sitting on our porch at home. Will he think to pick up his walking stick as he goes out to enjoy the sunshine for a bit? Will he think about the three of us sneaking off on a bus to find out just who is writing to Granny? Does he know about the mystery letters? I feel sure Granny and I will find a time to talk over the many questions swirling around in my head. But Popaw will probably just say, "That is none of your business, Half Pint."

Half Pint is his favorite nickname for me, and I don't mind a bit. He always reaches up and pretends to rub the hair on the top of my head when I start to ask too many questions.

A group of houses sitting back away from the two-lane road pulls my attention back to the passing landscape. They have no white siding, only weathered board siding and lots of chickens, pigs, and dogs running around. Every house has a small outhouse in the back, but that's not unusual. Only the Clarks and two other families in town have indoor plumbing with a restroom attached to the house. The day Elvie even mentions indoor plumbing is sure to start another heated argument. Not far from the small cluster of shacks, I notice a sign that reads Booker T. Washington Elementary School. How can that be? Another elementary school is less than five miles from my school, and I didn't even know it.

"Hey, look at that sign. Fran, have you ever heard about the Booker T. Washington Elementary school?"

"Yes, I have. And will you please keep your voice down? We can talk about that later." After traveling about thirty minutes in total silence, I can't bear it any longer.

"Hey, Elvie, what kind of snacks did you bring along?"

"There's peanut butter and jelly sandwiches, carrot slices, and some store-bought chocolate cookies. I brought enough for all of us, but I don't think we should start eating on the bus. What do you think, Fran?"

"Definitely not. We will look for a place to eat after we leave the library."

Well, Fran is taking her role of being in charge a little too seriously, but I have to admit she knew just what to say to the bus driver to get us on board. I can't wait to ask her what she would have said if the driver asked to see her letter of permission. One thing I know for sure, she isn't in the Junior class at school. As far as I can figure, she will start eighth grade in August. Of course, I don't actually know what grade is called the Junior class. But I am sure glad she decided to come along to the Austin Public Library.

Soon, the bus slows, and I notice a sign.

Welcome to Austin, Mississippi

1958 State Basketball Champions

Population 14, 061.

Now I know how Austin can afford a huge public library.

Franklin's population is 724, and we are just lucky to have our own post office. At first, the houses look pretty much like the homes in Franklin, except they are bigger with carports and probably indoor plumbing, too. We pass several gas stations, grocery stores, and a fancy restaurant named *Cracker Barrel*. I count five different churches and three drugstores. Then we pass the Austin Public Library. I have never seen such tall white columns in my entire life. There are at least twenty steps leading up to the front door. The bus doesn't stop.

"Hey, can we not get off here?" I lean over to get Fran's attention.

"Hush Ruby, I have a map, and we will have to walk about three blocks. We get off at the bus station."

I gain a new respect for my sister, who has given much thought to the trip details. We are jolted forward in our seats as the bus comes to a stop. The bus driver snarls a reminder that he had a schedule to keep, and the bus will depart for Franklin at 11:00. With a glare, he adds that he waits for no one. A sinking feeling in my stomach develops as I start down the aisle to follow Elvie and Fran. It is one thing to plan a secret trip, but now, I am losing some of my courage about carrying out the details. I have never seen Elvie this excited. He is enjoying the freedom of being away from his momma. With Fran in the lead, we leave the bus station and walk north toward the library.

As we walk down the sidewalk, something in a store window catches my eye. Inside I see a counter, like the one at Holt's Drugstore. I see little round seats that turn around and around in front of the counter. The sign outside says *Lambert's Soda Fountain, Whites only*. I have had a soda before, but I've never sat on a swirling seat.

"Ruby, come on! We have to keep moving to get to the library on time. Stay behind Elvie and concentrate. Quit looking around so much."

I have several remarks for Miss Honor Roll but think this was not the time or place. Austin has two hardware stores, a big post office, three drugstores, even a grocery store named Piggly Wiggly with more grocery carts than I have ever seen. When it's time to cross the street, I am glad to stay close because cars are zooming around. At last, I spot the tall white columns of the library. I race ahead of Elvie to see if Fran has a comment. She doesn't. Elvie holds to the iron rail that stretches up the steps, but I take two steps at a time. Fran and I both glance up at the big door leading into the library. I take a deep breath and open the door to the most marvelous place I have ever seen.

The tables and chairs are shiny and clean, and even the floor looks fancy and glowing. I hope my tennis shoes don't slip or slide. I can only imagine what Fran will say if I embarrass her, especially since she is trying so hard to be in charge. I know enough to look for the information sign, and I spy it before either Elvie or Fran.

"Fran, reference books are at the information place. Let's go this way." I whisper in my most grown-up voice. They follow me without a word, and I am determined to show Elvie Clark that he doesn't know everything about everything. The librarian stands up from her desk and looks over the top of her glasses. I take one step back. She doesn't smile, and her tone tells me she isn't pleased to see three kids in her workspace.

"Just what business do you three students have here today? Austin Public School finished classes last week. If any patron wants to check out material, I need to see a library card."

"We have a question about an APO zip code on an envelope we found," replied Fran.

"I can help you with that, but I still need to see your library card."

"We don't have library cards, but I am sixteen years old. Can you help me get one, please?"

"I can do that since you are over twelve, but your two friends will need to have an adult along to sign the permission card."

While Fran and the Reference Librarian fill out the card, I ask Elvie about the soda fountain. He says that he and his mom stopped there on another trip. He goes on to talk about milkshakes, chocolate sundaes, and even a banana split. "But Momma wouldn't let me sit at the counter because the swirly seats are dangerous for children. Hey, I got money for three cones of ice cream if Fran thinks we have time." Maybe she'll let us, but anyway, I am glad that Fran is here, or this whole trip would have been useless.

After about fifteen minutes of walking through the tall rows of books, Fran finds us and announces that she knows the long-awaited answer to our question. The APO stands for Vietnam. Granny has been getting letters from someone stationed in Vietnam. As we stared at each other, I asked myself exactly what to do with this information.

But more important than that is the time. I want to run out the door in the direction of the soda fountain. Fran reminds us that we need to find a clock to see how much time we have left before walking back to the bus station. Elvie says the courthouse is only one block over, and there is a giant clock tower outside the front door. As we leave the library, we see the clock high in the air. The hands point to 10:15. We have thirty minutes to do whatever we want and fifteen more before the bus leaves for home. Elvie mentions the soda fountain. Fran's eyes lit up almost as much as mine when we passed the store on our trip to the library.

Peanut butter and jelly sandwiches can wait. We head back two blocks and enter the store that has a delicious, sweet smell that reminds me of Granny's Christmas cookies. Elvie seems a little nervous as we head to the swirly seats at the counter. After three or four swirls around on my stool, I notice Fran giving me her big sister look. The young man at the counter smiles and asks to take our order. Elvie orders, saying we need three cones of ice cream. I notice the young man smiles at Fran when he asks what flavor she wants. Elvie is the only one with any money, so I wonder why the boy behind the counter is smiling at Fran. Fran has the silliest, weird smile on her face I have ever seen, and she asks him how many flavors are available. I choose chocolate, Elvie picks vanilla, and Fran just sits there with that odd grin.

"And what can I get for you today, young lady?"

"What is your favorite flavor?" Fran asks him.

"I like Pistachio, myself."

"Then I will have Pistachio ice cream. Thank you so much."

I know sure that Fran has no idea what Pistachio tastes like. Something else is going on here, and I couldn't care less as long as Elvie is paying. My stomach is growling as I lick the sweet chocolate-flavored cream. I make a few more swirls on my seat before Fran announces we have five minutes before we have to leave. As we leave the store, I remember to thank Elvie for the ice cream, but Fran doesn't. She's quiet, and she still has a goofy look on her face.

We get back to a park bench, and I want to sit and have a peanut butter sandwich. Fran says we have to get back to the bus station first and check our time. There is a water fountain beside the bench, and as we pass it, I notice a sign on the bottom of the fountain. *Whites Only*. People in Austin, Mississippi, sure don't think much of their Black neighbors. Where in the world do all the hard feelings between the Whites and the Blacks come from? Little do I know now, but before the summer of 1961 ends, I am to understand more about these strange feelings. I will learn more than I really want to know.

The ride back to Franklin is a real letdown for me. Fran looks out the window, seeming a thousand miles away. I am careful not to sit too close to Elvie because I know he will have too many questions about the Vietnam letter. I just as soon not hear his questions. I sure don't have any answers. We get back into town and get off the bus without anyone asking about the trip. We walk home without a word.

When we step up on the porch, I put my hand on Fran's shoulder and say, "Thanks."

She smiles and nods her head. We are extra careful not to let the screen door slam, and we tiptoe into the room to check on Popaw. He's asleep, so we start to make lunch as quietly as possible. Fran barely eats a bite of her bologna sandwich and even leaves several slices of the cucumber and onion we sliced. Oh well, I have to get busy and make some plans for the second serious conversation that Granny and I need to have soon.

I also want to find out more about the Booker T. Washington School and to see if anyone there knows about separate drinking fountains or that Blacks have to sit in the back two seats on the bus. Why hasn't Mr. Haley mentioned this in history class? I felt bad going into the soda fountain with a sign that says Whites only, but I didn't feel bad enough to pass up ice cream and a chance to twirl around on those round seats.

TEN

FOR WEEKS AFTER WE returned from the library, Fran and I did everything we could do to help around the house. I think it has a lot to do with a guilty conscience, but as far as we know, none of our lies have been uncovered. Every Sunday at church, Fran and I go out the side door, so we don't have to pass the pew where the Turners sit. If they mention seeing us on the bus, we know we'll be grounded for life. Elvie and his new friend Jesse Adams are usually not too far behind us, possibly for the same reason. Jessie is coming to Bible class with Elvie. He is a good reader. Preacher Brewer teaches the young people's class, and he's almost quit asking me to read aloud, so Elvie and Jessie have taken the lead. That's just fine by me. Fran's the top reader in our family. Besides, I have serious questions bothering me. Thinking too much always make me hungry, so my ears perk up when Preacher Brewer mentions the potluck dinner on the first Sunday in June.

While he is delivering a sermon about brotherly love, I decide I will make a trip down the road to share some brotherly love with the Booker T. Washington School students. If their school is out for the summer like my school, I will just look around and maybe talk to the school janitor. Granny always says if anyone has any questions about what happened at school, they should just ask the janitor.

Near the end of June, I finally have an afternoon free from weeding the garden, carrying laundry back and forth from the Clarks, and reading to Popaw. Of course, I enjoy the time with Popaw, reading about cowboys from the Wild West. Zane Grey is an author who can have you ducking bullets during the final shootout. But I need to get outside to clear the fog from my brain. Booker T. Washington, water fountains for Whites and Blacks, back seats in a bus, and a mystery soldier — all these ideas keep creating more and more questions. Where to find the answers is the real problem.

"Granny, can I walk over to Jesse Adams' pond with my fishing pole?"

"Now, Ruby Ann, it's too far for you to go alone. How about asking Elvie Clark to go along? You know the preacher has been talking about brotherly love lately. He will jump at a chance to go fishing."

"He can't even bait his own hook. I might as well stay home."

"Fran has been sitting out under the back trees for over an hour. Maybe she will take her book along and keep you company. She doesn't give a hoot about fishing. You'd not have to spend any time baiting her hook."

"Granny. I am almost nine years old. When are you and Momma gonna trust me to go places alone?"

"I do trust you, but I'm just trying to keep you safe, baby girl. Now, just to prove I trust you, take this letter down to the post office. It's a payment to Sears, and I want it postmarked today."

"Sure, I can do that. I might even have a chance to look under some big rocks for some nightcrawlers. Popaw always says they make the best fish bait. By the end of summer, when it's not so hot, maybe he'll feel like going fishing with me."

"That is possible. But ya know, you could teach Elvie how to bait his hook in the meantime."

Walking down the dirt road between our house and town, I start to think about the mystery letter from Vietnam. If I am brave enough, I can just ask Granny about the letter. Has there been only one letter? Granny still walks to the mailbox around 1 o'clock every day. I notice she often puts the mail in one of her apron pockets and then walks to her bedroom before she opens it. Adults often talk about trust, but the older I get, it seems like many adults aren't so trustworthy. But Granny is, and I know that for sure.

As I walk into the post office, I look for the mail slot. Something else catches my eye. A new display case with different American flags and pictures inside is hanging beside the front door. As I study the photos inside, I realize they are all soldiers. The heading in bold black letters over the display reads Franklin County's Proud Sons of War. All the men are soldiers who live within a hundred-mile radius of Franklin County. These soldiers are solemn faced, looking so handsome in their uniforms, and they are all serving in

Vietnam.

One name caught my eye--Kendrick. One soldier is named Ted Kendrick. I feel numb, and I can hardly breathe. As I look at the man's face, I see a pair of eyes that look familiar. But I don't see my eyes, I see Fran's. I sit down and lean against the wall. I still have Granny's letter in my hand. I almost wad it up as I slump to the floor, trying to make some sense of the picture in the case. That soldier has the eyes of my sister Fran, but not my eyes, not my chin shape, or anything that resembles me at all. That soldier could be my father, Ted Kendrick, a soldier who might have been writing to my Granny. That's just fine with me. What has he ever done for our family anyway? Remembering the letter in my hand, I smooth it out and walk to the mail slot. Why would my dad write Granny but not my mom? Why would he not come to see his own family?

"Excuse me, young lady, I need to drop my letter in the mail slot. Are you finished?"

"Sorry, I don't mean to block you. I'm just thinking."

As I drop the Sears payment in the slot and head out the door, I stopped. I can't go home. Not yet. Too many thoughts are in my head, so I start walking in the opposite direction. As I got close to my school, I decide to stop by the playground. School's out, so no students are around. I know the janitor can't help with these serious matters. All the teachers are gone, so I have to make some plans.

As I sit on the merry-go-round with my head in my hands, I take several deep breaths and decide to talk to Fran.

She was a real trooper to help Elvie and me on the bus trip. I want her to come with me to the post office to see Ted's picture. Ted's picture. I can't say *my dad's* picture. He looks like the same man in Mom's wedding picture. I refuse to think the picture hanging in the post office is a picture of the same man who planted trees on the day we were born. What are the chances there is another Ted Kendrick in a hundred-mile radius of Franklin? It isn't impossible. I'll see what Fran thinks, and then maybe she and I both can talk to Granny. Even on those days or weeks when Mom retreats to her bedroom, Granny says we can always ask her anything. Granny tells us Momma needs time to herself, and she will talk when she's ready.

"We can't all be the same, and your mom is a very private person. Now me, I'm gonna let you know what is on my mind, even if ya don't want to hear it. And, I promise you girls, you can talk to me about anything, and I will give you an honest answer if I can."

While I'm sitting in the swing, I wonder if there are times when Granny can't give an honest answer. My head hurts from all this thinking.

"Hey, Ruby, what are you doing sitting here on the playground all by yourself?" Elvie Clark is the last person on earth I want to talk to, so I take off running. Thank goodness he doesn't try to follow me. I run until I hear the screen door slam behind me.

Although Granny's fried chicken is my favorite supper, I find it hard to wait until the dishes are washed and dried before asking Fran to meet me by the trees in the backyard.

"I knew something was wrong when you only got one helping of creamed potatoes and gravy. I picked up one of Granny's quilts and a couple of books from the shelf in case someone decides to join us," Fran said.

After she spread the quilt on the grass, I hit Fran with my bombshell. "Ted Kendrick is a soldier in Vietnam, and I think Granny is getting letters from him."

"Ruby, your imagination is going wild. That makes no sense at all."

"Yeah, his picture is hanging in the post office. Maybe you can see for yourself when you go down there."

"You don't even remember what our dad looks like. How can you be so sure?"

"You look like him, and what are the chances that Granny would know another soldier in Vietnam? I saw pictures, and it's the only explanation that makes any sense. You know it."

"If you are so sure, go get Granny right now and ask her. Are you ready to ask her that question?"

"I will when I get ready. Do you think we should ask Mom first? Why wouldn't he write to his own wife instead of Granny? Will Popaw get upset if he knows about the letters? Maybe he already knows."

"I'm sure Popaw doesn't know about the letters. He never wanted to hear my dad's name after he left town and deserted his family. Do you know what being so nosy about Granny's letters can do to our family? Please, Ruby, let it all go. What does it matter if Granny has been talking to our dad? He doesn't want to see any of us, that's for sure. Please, Ruby. You can't go blabbing to Mom and Granny about some photograph of a man that might not even be who you think he is."

"I know who it is, and you do too. You're just afraid to find out the truth."

For a minute, Fran's lip starts to quiver, and her eyes look full of tears. She doesn't say another word for a long time. Finally, she stands up, grabs the quilt and the two books, and marches to the house. She leaves me on the grass where I landed when she pulled the quilt from under me.

Am I brave enough to talk to Granny alone? I am, but the time has to be right, and Fran and Mom can't be anywhere around. Granny and I will get our fishing poles, and I know before too long I will have the answers to all the questions that have puzzled me over for months. But the time for fishing never comes—at least at least for months.

When Granny goes to tell Popaw that his breakfast is ready on August 2, 1961, she finds that he has died in his sleep. Granny doesn't say a word until after lunch on that sad day. She just sits on the porch in her rocker and stares down the road, almost like she could see something out there that none of us can see. Fran takes off running to the church to find Preacher Brewer while I sit on the porch steps waiting for something but not knowing what or who might come along to help make sense of my world. Momma holds Granny's hand as she sits beside her, but there aren't words for a long spell.

My Popaw died from a massive heart attack. The doctor said he had no pain and left this world peacefully. Pain is all that is left in this house for a long time. Now there is a funeral to plan, and many people are coming and going.

One thing that seems important to our neighbors is food. Two of our closest neighbors bring fried chicken wrapped up in a dishcloth in a picnic basket by lunch that day. Others bring fresh biscuits, creamed potatoes, white gravy, chocolate cake, and sugar cookies, but no one ever calls us to the table. Granny always says it's impolite to gather at the table unless the cook announces that all is ready. The smell of that food is all through the house, but it doesn't seem right to enjoy good food when Popaw isn't there to say a blessing. When the word spreads that Popaw passed, our screen door opens and closes more than ever before. Food, food, and more food shows up at our door.

Fran and I go outside while the preacher talks in a muffled voice to Momma and Granny. We sit on a quilt under the Crepe Myrtle trees and say, "No, thank you," every time someone tries to get us to eat something. I just want to hear Granny say that everything will be all right. That didn't happen that day or the next. But polite or not, a person can only go so long without eating, so Fran and I did eat before bedtime that second day. Momma says it would be better for us to spend the night over at Mrs. Clark's house. This isn't my choice but having a dead body in the house isn't my choice either. The undertaker can't come until early the next morning, so Popaw's body will be prepared for the burial that night after Fran and I are carted off to the Clarks. No questions here. I trust Momma and Granny to do all the preparations, and I am determined to keep my eyes down and my mouth shut as much as possible.

The next day, Elvie informs Fran and me that the undertaker will send some men to take Popaw's measurements for a casket. I sure am glad that happened while Fran and I were asleep in Mrs. Clark's spare bedroom. Elvie is extra nice to me for almost two days. All he wants to talk about is what he knows about the job of an undertaker, grave diggers, and even what will happen after Popaw's body is taken to the funeral parlor. I tell him we went to a funeral parlor when Granny's mother died. Actually, I was only three, and Fran was seven, but I had seen some pictures as proof that I was there.

One time Granny showed me a picture of her, her brothers, sisters, and her mother in front of the open casket with Granny's daddy. That photo is so weird. I am glad Granny put it in the top of her closet. Pictures of people in a casket don't seem like a good tradition. Thank goodness Granny says we didn't have to have any photos made around Popaw's casket.

The night before the funeral, Preacher Brewer and his family came over to eat supper. He asks Granny about special songs that she wants the congregation to sing at the funeral. I'm glad she picked *Amazing Grace* because Popaw used to sing that when we were swinging on the front porch. Fran's favorite is *Sing to Me of Heaven*. Granny and Momma pick *What a Friend We Have in Jesus*.

Finally, the day of the funeral arrives. Mom says we must all wear dark clothes. Granny's two sisters and several other family members arrive at our house not long after breakfast. They all sit around the kitchen table and drink three pots of coffee and even manage to get Granny and Mom to smile, telling stories of living with my Great-Grandparents. Several of these stories included Popaw's family too. Granny had not heard from his brothers, but she hoped to see them at the funeral.

As we get to the church that morning, everyone seems to want to hug a lot and then cry quite a bit too. Tissues are being passed around as the family waits under the shade trees while others go straight into the church. The funeral director thinks the family should walk into the services in some kind of order, so Fran and I wait to be told where we should stand. Granny, her sisters, and then Momma line up. Momma is holding firmly to my and Fran's hands. Behind us is one of Popaw's brothers, the only one who is able to attend. He looks so much like my Popaw that all I can do is stare at him until Mom jerks my face around for a quick kiss on the cheek. I am glad to have mom holding my hand to lead me to my seat while I keep my eyes on the floor.

The songs are sung, and a few good memories enter my mind as I think about sitting on the front porch swing, singing those same tunes. I hear words about heaven, angels, and hope. My only hope for the future is that our family will stay strong and never need to leave the home where I have lived my entire life. Many times, Popaw reminded Fran and me about what strong roots the Moore family have in Franklin. There is no way Ted Kendrick can be as strong as my Popaw...NO WAY. He doesn't know a thing about how to make strong roots.

Soon everyone begins to exit the building as they pass the casket to say farewell. Granny and Mom have red splotches on their cheeks. As they cry, so do Fran and me. Finally, we all stand up, and Granny wants to hold hands with Fran and me as we walk by the casket. She whispers something to Popaw as we stop for a while. I hope he can hear what she said, and I hope he knows how much we will all miss him. This is a hard, long day. The only way I know to get through it is to keep quiet and keep my eyes down. Yes, my eyes are swollen, and my cheeks are splotchy. Everywhere I look, there are sad faces. Granny says a good cry can cleanse the soul, but my soul feels empty, not clean. Mom lets Fran and me sleep on the floor in her room. Granny brings in a chair and sits with us for a while. One of the strongest parts of the Moore family tree is gone. Now we have nothing to do but stay close to those left behind.

The summer of 1961 brings many changes to our family. Momma has a part-time job working at Holt's Drugstore. With Mom at work, Fran and I have extra chores inside and outside the house. The chickens have to be fed, eggs have to be gathered, and turnip greens have to be picked, even though both of us hate the look and taste of this "good-for-you" food. Several years ago, Popaw told us about a famous person named Popeye the Sailor Man who eats greens all the time. He's one of the strongest people alive. Elvie says he never heard of Popeye, which makes me want to prove him wrong. Preacher Brewer has heard of him, but he told us Popeye isn't a real person, just a legend. Anyway, I hate any food that looks like grass and has a terrible smell when it's boiled in water.

Fran and I also have to wash supper dishes every night because Momma is tired after working three days a week. Granny always reminds me to carry water out back to the trees, but she seldom walks along with me. As Fran and I carry pails of water to the Crepe Myrtles and our oak tree, I often bring up the topic of Ted Kendrick and the picture that still is hanging in the post office.

"Ruby, forget all about that picture. If you mention it to Mom or Granny and they start crying again, I'm going to tell them you made up that crazy story about a Vietnam soldier. I couldn't care less about a picture that Ted Kendrick might have in the Post Office."

"Fran, you're crazy! I saw it myself about a month ago. Do you want to walk down there with me and see for yourself? Of course, you don't because I know you are lying. I can see it in your eyes."

"You're crazy if you think I'm going to let you worry Granny and Momma about someone who doesn't care a thing about us. Just forget it, and keep your mouth shut."

I stick my tongue out at Fran. I have to find time to talk to Granny. She will tell me the truth. One of Preacher Brewer's favorite scripture is, "You shall know the truth, and it will set you free." I decide to wait until after Christmas to find out more about Ted Kendrick. But the Booker T. Washington School for Colored People is barely twelve miles from Franklin, Mississippi. I will find some answers next Saturday. Knowing the truth has to be a good thing. How can I face the things ahead if I can't be honest about the things around me? There is no way I will ask for Fran's help because I'll keep my mouth shut as far as she is concerned. I don't want to make Granny or Mom upset either. I'll be patient about the picture in the post office, but I'm determined to learn more about another school barely twelve miles past mine that no one ever mentions to me.

ELEVEN

WHEN I FINISH MY chores on Saturday, I grab a cane pole, a can of worms, and a small tackle box that belonged to Popaw. I ask Momma if I can go over to Jesse's pond and spend the day fishing. She says I can if Fran agrees to take the clothes over to Mrs. Clarks' in my place. After Fran marks the calendar for my two Saturdays in a row for clean clothes delivery, she agrees without asking why.

I start the long walk out of town with some peanut butter and crackers, two apples, and a quart jar of cold water. If I stop every hour for about five minutes to rest, maybe I can get there and back before dark. Thank goodness few people are out traveling on Saturday, and those who are don't notice me. When I hear a car approaching, I get over in the side ditch, but I am determined to walk until about noon before I stop to eat a bite. I hide my fishing stuff behind a deserted shop downtown. When the sun is overhead, I see my first sign. The sign reads *County Rd 213 to Booker T. School 5 miles.*

Just as I spy County Road 213, I hear a car approaching from behind, moving slowly.

"And just where are you going, young lady?"

I freeze in my tracks. Preacher Brewer's warnings of

wayward strangers are echoing in my brain. Granny's stories about missing children springs to mind. As I'm contemplating my next move, the car stops beside me.

"Ruby Kendrick, you look like you could use a ride." Mr. Haley flashes his great smile.

I thought schoolteachers spend every weekend grading papers. Two of my teachers let it slip that they have a second job. The only teacher at Franklin Elementary who is caught up on paper grading and doesn't have another job happens to be riding down this road. Just my luck!

"You certainly are a long way from home. Where are you headed?" Mr. Haley asked.

"If I tell you the truth, will you promise not to tell?"

"As long as you aren't running away from home or up to some mischief, I suppose I can keep that secret for one of my favorite students at Franklin Elementary."

"Being curious is a good thing, don't you think?" I laughed nervously and gulp. "I remember times at school when you wouldn't answer questions just because we need to dig out answers by ourselves. At first, I thought you really might not know the answer, but then my second thought was you wanted us to work a little harder and not take the easy way out."

"Ruby, I have never known you to take the easy way out in anything you have tried to do. Now, you still haven't answered my question. What in the world are you doing this far from home walking on the side of the road? And I want the truth, young lady."

"The truth is I want to find out about another elementary school that is right down that next road. You probably need to know that Momma thinks I am fishing today at Jesse Adam's pond. I have another story about getting lost that I could tell you, but I can't lie because you are my favorite teacher."

"Flattery isn't necessary, Ruby. You know it's rather dangerous for you to be out here alone walking down this road. You could have stopped by the school and got some answers about Booker T. Washington School. Hop in the car. I'm on my way to deliver this box of books to that school. Maybe you can get some of your questions answered today without having to walk all the way."

As I walk around the front of Mr. Haley's car, I notice immediately that his car is even older than ours. I know that he doesn't have a wife or kids, so maybe teaching school doesn't pay as much as Granny thinks. To hear her talk about college, she thinks a four-year degree is a ticket to success.

"Wow, this is my lucky day after all. That is, it will be lucky if you agree to keep this trip our secret. Mr. Haley, why does this school need our old books? That one on top of that box is one we used two years ago in history. Those books were worn out then. Can't they afford to get books with tax money? You told us that one time. Don't they pay their taxes?"

"One question at a time, Ruby. Slow down and take a breath. Yes, the people who live in this community pay taxes, just like everybody in Franklin does. Their tax base is not as high because their income is lower, so Franklin Schools helps them out as much as we can."

"I have never heard about a tax base, but if they need those ole raggedy books, I kinda feel sorry for kids in that school. You know, I remember something that I noticed when I went to Austin. We went into a soda fountain, and a sign said no Colored people allowed. I saw two drinking fountains on the street, one for White people and one for Colored people. Do you think that the Austin Colored people have a low tax base too? If ya ask me, keeping up two drinking fountains is a real waste of money. Granny says some people have no idea how to save money because they waste a bunch. At our house, we don't waste anything. Sorry about talking so much. I will try to listen more now."

"What you say does hold a lot of truth. Booker T. School has only a few students that we could serve at the Franklin Schools much more effectively. They could bus them into Franklin if the people of Franklin would welcome them. But that is not going to happen, so you and I might as well talk about something more pleasant."

I want to ask why the people of Franklin wouldn't welcome the students of Booker T. Washington, but I decide to practice my listening skills, not my talking-too-much skills. As we cross a wooden bridge and head along a small dirt road, I notice cotton fields on either side of the road.

In Franklin, Mississippi, many people farm cotton or soybeans. Most people work on a farm or at the Taylor Furniture Factory, two miles outside the city limits. I don't see any businesses as we get closer to the school. Twenty or so small frame houses are visible, and just beyond, I spot a larger white building with a flag by the front porch. I also spy a giant oak tree with two bag swings. I hope I can check those out.

"Here we are, Ruby. Wanna help me get these boxes into the school? I will need to find someone in the office to sign this delivery form. You can look around the classrooms if you want."

As we approach the five narrow steps leading up to the school building, I see the peeling paint around the front door and a side window broken out. Someone has made a repair with some cardboard and tape. The door isn't locked. Mr. Haley holds the door with his back to let me go in first. The wooden floor creaks as we walk down a long hall. The echo of the door closing behind us makes me want to stay close to Mr. Haley. I glance into several classrooms as I follow my teacher.

Clearly, this school doesn't have as many students as Franklin Elementary, but student desks and a chalkboard hanging on the wall behind a teacher's desk are what I expect to see. Pictures of George Washington and Abraham Lincoln look exactly like the ones in the back of Mr. Haley's classroom. I almost bump into him when he finally slows down because I spot a big picture above the classroom door. I have never seen a picture of a black man hanging in our school, but the name printed below caught my eye--Booker T. Washington, 1856-1915. The picture shows a light-colored black man, dressed in a bowtie and a suit like Preacher Brewer wears almost every Sunday. He is holding an open book. Mr.

Washington looks like a teacher with his staring eyes and serious expression.

"Ruby, put that box on the floor by the door. What do you think of Mr. Washington's picture?"

"I can think of a few questions I'd like to ask him, but I notice he died in 1915. He must have been a rich man to have a nice big picture with glass over it like that."

"He gave a lot of his money to build schools for Black children in the South. Remind me, and I will share his autobiography with you when school starts back."

"Sure, if I can remember. Can I go back out front and swing on the bag swing until you are finished?"

I walk ever so slowly down the creaking old wood floor, thinking of another hall I walked down before Popaw's funeral. Maybe it's because the building is so quiet that I remember that day. I know I shouldn't run in the hall of any school, but I was running by the time I got to the door. When I get outside, I am breathing so hard I think my chest might pop right open. I bend over to catch my breath and to tell myself to calm down when I hear crying. Someone is sitting on the ground under the big oak tree. Walking with tiny baby steps, I creep closer. This person has her head down. I see dark black curls resting on a set of bony knees. A small girl about my size is curled into a ball. She wears shorts and a tee shirt.

"Hey, whatcha crying about? Are you hurt? My teacher is in the building if you want me to get him."

As I get closer, the girl wipes tears with the back of her hand. For the first time in my life, I am talking to a black person, but crying is crying no matter who it's coming from. I'd heard Popaw say once that we all bleed the same red blood. I know he was talking about his daddy fighting in World War I. Funny, I should remember that now, but I suppose we all cry the same wet tears when we are sad, too.

She rose to her feet. "No, please don't go get anybody."

We just stand there, waiting for the other to say something. She puts both hands behind her back and looks at the ground. She is a little taller than me, but she's skinny, like a bean pole.

"What do you have behind your back?" I ask.

"Nothing!"

"Well, I can see something you are holding, but if you don't want to tell me, that's your business. If you are not hurt, I'm just going to go wait for my teacher over there."

As I turn to walk toward the car, the girl runs right past me and sits on the porch step of the school.

"What are you doing here at my school? My mom works in the office, and I never seen you here before. Never even seen any White kids here before. What's up?"

"I might tell ya why I am here if you will tell me why you were sitting over there bawling like a baby?"

"Crying doesn't make me a baby. I was reading a letter from my dad and started missing him a lot."

"I'm Ruby, and I live in Franklin about twelve miles up the main highway. Where is your daddy anyway?"

"I know where Franklin is, but what are you doing here?" What business does your teacher have at a Black school? Is your daddy a teacher?"

"Hey, slow down. You ask more questions than I do. I rode over here with Mr. Haley, my history teacher from Franklin Elementary. I know hardly anything about my daddy. How long has your daddy been gone? You never told me where he went."

"He went to fight in the Vietnam War almost two years ago. He writes to my momma and me every month, but I am afraid he won't even know me when he gets back. Thomas says that he might never get to come back home because the President is sending more troops over there now."

"Well, I don't know Thomas, but I wouldn't listen to anyone saying crazy stuff like that."

"Thomas is my big brother. He's almost thirteen, and he thinks he knows everything. He says he's the man of the house now that Daddy's gone."

"Boys think they know everything about everything. Has Thomas ever walked all the way to Franklin by himself? I left this morning coming here by myself. Woulda made it too, but Mr. Haley offered me a ride."

"Your momma lets you take off walking by yourself, and you aren't scared? Wow! Why in the world do ya wanna come here? Nothin' much here. Maybe thirty families, and this whole school only has forty-three kids. During harvest times, we have barely twenty."

"I didn't exactly tell Momma I was coming here, but I wasn't a bit afraid. Once I went on a bus trip to Austin with my sister and her friend, and we solved a mystery. You want to hear about my bus trip?"

Before the girl can get another word out, Mr. Haley comes out on the school porch. He looks surprised to see me sitting right outside the door.

"Ruby, come on. We need to head home. Hello, young lady, I am Dan Haley, and I teach school at Franklin Elementary. I bet you and Ruby are about the same age. Has she been telling you what an outstanding teacher I am?"

For the first time, I saw a big grin on her face as she nodded her head. She stands up and runs toward the tree. I yell at her.

"Hey, you didn't tell me your name."

She stops in her tracks, turns around, and answers. "It's Emma, Emma Parks, but my friends call me crybaby sometimes."

I hear her laugh as she goes back toward the tree. She waves several times as we start to back up. I like her laughter, and I certainly understand her crying about a daddy that is away. I hope we will meet again. Little do I know that we'll meet soon, and she will be crying.

I yell back to her. "Maybe Mr. Haley will let me come back with him next time. Gotta go. I'm going to say a prayer that your daddy gets to come home soon. Bye."

Mr. Haley probably thinks I'm sick because I don't have much to say on the trip home. I'm thinking about Emma and Thomas alone at home with their mom while their daddy is overseas in a war. I don't know much about Booker T. Washington School, but I know only too well a family without a daddy. Mr. Haley informs me I shouldn't make any more trips on foot without my momma's permission. I say 'Okay.' Actually, I say 'Yes, sir' because I know how teachers light up when they hear those words.

TWELVE

THAT SCHOOL YEAR STARTS the same as always. We get off the bus, go straight to the gym, and listen to the same set of rules read over the speaker by Mr. Dunlap, the same school principal who has been here since Momma was in school. Each grade from first grade through twelfth grade has an assigned area in the gym. I see Elvie and Jesse sitting at the top row, so I sit on the bottom. Maybe, just maybe, this will be the year that Elvie doesn't yell out my name and wave both hands in the air.

Fran, who has not been speaking to me lately, sits with her Junior High friends. I have a fluttering feeling in my stomach. Nothing new. Granny calls it the first-day jitters, and she always says new beginnings and new possibilities can make anyone a little skittish.

I sit beside Betty Mangrum, a girl who has been in my homeroom for three straight years. She wears shiny new saddle oxfords, a ruffled skirt, and a white blouse buttoned to the top. We don't have much in common, but she looks as nervous as I felt. My brotherly kindness Bible lesson kicks in, so I start a conversation.

"Hey, Betty, you look nice today. Are you ready for the

new school year?"

"I guess I am. I was nervous when I heard that we might have some Black kids at our school this year. Have you heard that rumor? My uncle from Chicago says that all the schools there are already integrated, and I wonder if our school will bus the Booker T. Washington students here this year. Since segregation is against the law, my daddy tells me it's only a matter of time before Blacks come to our schools. Does that make you nervous, Ruby?"

I'm about to tell her I have no idea what segregation means, but instead, I just shake my head and pretend to be interested in the enrollment forms the teachers are giving us. Betty leaves when Mr. Dunlap announces that all music and band students need to report to the main office. Then Elvie yells out my name and waves both hands like the American flag in all its glory. He and Jesse move down and tell me they plan to try out for the basketball team. Unless Elvie has been working on his athletic skills over the summer, he will probably end up in study hall with me. Some things never change.

Betty and I sit beside each other in the lunchroom, and I'm so glad she doesn't bring up anything about the Booker T. Washington students. We compare class schedules and discover we have homeroom with Mr. Haley and two other classes together. She has all kinds of questions about Jesse Adams. When I tell her I don't really know him, she insists that I get Elvie to introduce her. I almost swallow my gum when she calls Elvie my boyfriend. But when she says he told her that himself, I become furious. I can hardly wait until school is over to give him a piece of my mind. But what happens next makes me forget about Elvie Clark and Jesse Adams.

Mr. Dunlap's voice comes over the loudspeaker. He announces the Booker T. Washington School is on fire. He dismisses school early so the bus drivers and male teachers can help put out the fire. The lady teachers are to stay with all bus riders until parents can come by the school.

Back we go to the gym to wait. While I wait, I wonder about Emma and her family. The last time I had seen Emma she was crying because she missed her dad. I wonder what happens to kids who don't have parents to care for them. Emma hadn't mentioned any grandparents, but we talked barely for thirty minutes. I pray for the Booker T. Washington School and try not to worry about things that haven't happened yet. Before I can get a good prayer started in my mind, Elvie comes bounding down the bleachers and grabs me by the hand.

"Come on with me, Ruby. Your mom says you and Fran are supposed to ride home with my mom and me." Before I can ask any questions, I see Fran walking in our direction. She has a frown on her face.

"The office got word that we are to wait at Mrs. Clark's house until mom gets off work at 5:00."

"Why can't we just go home and stay with Granny?"

"Why can't you just do as you're told? I didn't ask any questions, but the message says mom will be there to pick us up after work. Come on. Follow Elvie."

On the ride to Elvie's house, the only person in a cheery mood is Mrs. Clark. She says she heard the fire is minor, and no one has been injured. Franklin's Fire Department is one of the best in the county. All the volunteers arrived in less than thirty minutes to put out the fire that started in the boiler room. She couldn't imagine why the school still used an ancient boiler for hot water.

I'm not about to tell her that the school can't even afford new books. If I do, the next thing out of somebody's mouth would be to ask how I know about Booker T. Washington's textbooks. Besides, I can't get a word in edgewise with all the valuable information Mrs. Clark shares about the latest news in Franklin Society. Even Elvie rolls his eyes when she mentions how much money she donates to the Fire Department. She helps personally in every fundraiser.

Graham crackers and cold milk make the afternoon pass quickly as we try to be polite and wait for mom. While Fran helps clean up the kitchen with Mrs. Clark, Elvie and I sit on the front porch swing. It doesn't seem like a good time to bring up what Betty said earlier, so instead, I tell Elvie that I met a girl who goes to school at Booker T. Washington this summer. At first, he doesn't believe me, but he has lots of questions when I swear him to secrecy about my trip and mention her father in Vietnam.

"Ruby, why don't you just ask questions if you want to find out about the school for Black kids? That was a dangerous thing to do, walking down a busy highway."

"I can take care of myself, Elvie Clark. Just what do you know about Booker T. Washington School?"

"Well, I know that our government has passed a Civil Rights Act that says all kids should be able to get a good education no matter the color of their skin. Have you ever heard of a man named Martin Luther King, Jr.? He makes speeches on TV. Just last week, he said our country must find a peaceful way to do away with Blacks and Whites being separate in our country. He sure has made a lot of people mad. Jessie's daddy said there might even be a war worse than Vietnam."

"Well, a country can't be fighting two wars at the same time. There won't be enough soldiers to go around."

"Ruby, girls don't know anything about soldiers and war. That is a subject just for boys and men."

"For your information, I know two different men who are fighting in Vietnam right now. And I know about Vietnam battles because I've read some letters that soldiers have sent home."

I'm glad that mom drove up before I got any deeper in telling half-truths or lies about Vietnam letters. I hope to read Emma's dad's letter, and maybe, I will get to talk to Granny about her mystery soldier before too long. I may even let Elvie read Granny's letter just to prove him wrong about what girls know about the world.

At the supper table, mom says that the fire at Booker T. Washington destroyed over half the school. Luckily, the school isn't in session since most men and older kids are still working the cotton crops. Their school year doesn't start until after harvest, usually mid-October. She heard that the Franklin School Board called a special meeting next week to decide if the district will rebuild the school building.

"Why in the world would they build a new school for barely forty students?"

"Oh, I think there are more students in that school, Ruby. What makes you think there are around forty kids?" asks Granny.

Just as quick as a wink, another lie pops out of my mouth. It's almost scary how easy I can think up a lie. The world around me often makes no sense, so it's easier to make up details that do make sense. Honestly, my secrets are getting harder and harder to keep straight. Before too long, I will fess up to the truth. But not today.

"Mr. Haley told us about the Booker T. Washington School last year when we were talking about Civil Rights and Vietnam. He told us about Martin Luther King Jr. and how he makes speeches about getting Blacks and Whites to get along without fighting."

"I'm so proud of what you are learning, Ruby. Mr. King is a preacher who has wonderful ideas about what is good for our country. You need to listen to Mr. Haley. He is one of our best teachers at Franklin School."

Oh dear, Martin Luther King Jr. is a preacher, and here I sit telling lies about all I know about him. I understand what Preacher Brewer says about the truth, but then he doesn't have to put up with a know-it-all like Elvie Clark. I only hope the truth will set me free from all the lies that keep popping out of my mouth.

The rest of the school week passes by quickly after the fire scare at the Black school. We still have no word about the students from Booker T. Washington's School, but Emma, Thomas, and their mother sure are on my mind. I need to talk to someone. I bet Mr. Haley will help, but today when I went to his room after school, he wasn't there.

After several weeks, I decide to talk to Granny about my concerns. She always helps me make sense of the hard times in my life. Why not now? Well, because I will have to admit how I met Emma in the first place. But come what may, I can't wait another day to talk to someone about my worries. Maybe I can be brave enough to bring up the mystery Vietnam letter, too.

Saturday morning after breakfast, I ask Granny if we can take a quilt and have a picnic for lunch out under the Crepe Myrtle trees in the backyard. Momma and Fran are cleaning Mrs. Clark's house for the Daughters of the American Revolution Tea on Sunday. Since they will be gone, this is the perfect time for a long talk. The word confession might be a better label for this time together. Granny says this is a fine suggestion.

"Are you sure you feel like going on this picnic, Ruby? You have been so quiet lately and barely ate any supper last night."

"I'm okay, Granny. I need to ask you something important, and I don't want Momma or Fran to listen."

"Well, you can ask me anything. I promise to listen and keep it a secret. First, let's get some picnic food together. Your Popaw always said sweet tea is the best thing to have in your hand when questions are swirling around in your head."

"I miss Popaw this time of the year. We used to walk out in the soybean field so he could pop open a pod and look at the bean inside. Of course, we stopped every so often to pull a weed, too. He would ask me what I thought about the moisture in the bean. I pretended to know what he was talking about, and he said he needed my help in deciding when to harvest those beans. That made me feel important. You miss him too, don't you, Granny?"

"I sure do, child, from the time my feet hit the floor until I fall asleep at night. We were married 65 years. I miss him something terrible. But I have you, Fran, and your momma to remind me of my blessings every day. And a picnic on a sunny day is a blessing, too. Let's get ready to go. Get a pillow along with that quilt. I probably need to prop up against a tree for this important talk we're gonna have. That pillow will help cushion this old back of mine."

After almost thirty minutes of loading up, we walk out the back door. A gentle breeze and the warmth of the sun coming through the leaves feel just right. The main sound I hear is leaves rustling on tree branches as the wind blows. I also hear tree frogs making a chirping noise. My heart is beating kinda fast. I can hear the pounding in my ears.

Confession is good for the soul, Preacher Brewer says, but he didn't mention what it does to your heart.

Granny sits with her skirt tucked up under her legs and takes off her shoes. She says the feel of a cool breeze on her bare feet makes her smile. She closes her eyes and leans her head back on the tree trunk. I am afraid she might go to sleep.

"I'm really thirsty now, Granny. Are you about ready for a glass of tea?"

"No. I just want to sit here a spell and enjoy being outside. But I promise to listen, Ruby. Whenever you get ready to talk, just let me know."

Maybe it has only been two or three minutes, but it seems like an eternity before I can muster up just the right words. Where should I start? Maybe I can leave out the part about the bus trip to Austin. I have to confess the road trip to Booker T. Washington since I'm concerned about Emma and her family. How concerned am I about this man who happened to be my father? Granny knows more about him than I do, for sure. He hasn't shown concern for our family for such a long time. Or had he, and I just don't know? Out of the blue comes my first question.

"Are my momma and daddy divorced?"

Granny's eyes pop open, and she sits up straight. "No. What would cause you to ask a question like that?"

After taking a deep breath and gathering all the courage I have, I replied, "I know you've been getting letters from a soldier in Vietnam. I saw a picture of Ted Kendrick in the post office, and he is in Vietnam. When married people have kids and don't live together, that usually means they are divorced. Why would my daddy write to you and not to my momma unless they are divorced, and he knows she doesn't want to talk to him? Why did he leave us anyway? Fran says he probably has another family somewhere else and never wants to see us again. Then, why does he write to you? Another thing I don't understand is...."

"Whoa! Slow down, Ruby. One question at a time. Your parents are not divorced, and as to why Ted does not live here, you must talk to your mom about that. Okay, Little Miss Know-It-All, your dad has sent money to me every month since he left. Your Popaw would have no part of that, so I agreed not to tell him, but your momma knows all about it. He does not have another family, as far as I know. But this I am sure of, he loves you and Fran and your momma. Here is a question for you, young lady. Just what do you know about my letters from Ted? Please don't tell me you've been looking through my chest at the foot of my bed."

"Oh no, Granny, I know better than that. I saw a letter with a special APO number on it. It came in the mail one day when mom and I stopped out at the mailbox. Mr. Haley told me that the letter with that kind of address was from someone in the military. You have always told Fran and me to ask questions if we don't understand something."

"Well, maybe I am the one you should have asked, not Mr. Haley."

"Granny, I want to believe you, but it sure is hard to believe a person could love someone without coming more than eight years to see them."

"Ruby, your dad wants to see you and Fran, but your momma just doesn't think that is good right now. Sometimes adults make mistakes, and they get so sad and need to live apart. Your dad has sent money to help us, and he will come back when he knows he is welcome. Sorry, that is all I can say now."

"Well, you can just tell him that he is not welcome, and we don't need him."

Then I start to cry so hard my shirt gets wet. When I begin to blow my nose on my shirttail, Granny gets up slowly and hugs me tight to her chest. We stand there until Granny says she has to sit back down. She takes my hand, and I sit down in her lap. I am so glad she has a big lap. Sometimes, no matter how upset I am, my stomach just starts growling, and I gotta eat.

"Child, it sounds like your stomach is trying to tell us something,"

We eat our peanut butter and jelly sandwiches and several apple slices. Granny says it's time to gather our picnic and get to the house. She promises that soon we will have a family meeting, and I will get answers to my important questions. I don't remember Emma and her family until I go to bed. My picnic with Granny had been a flop. I have very few answers about my dad, and I didn't even mention my friend who has no school or daddy. Some friend I am.

THIRTEEN

NOVEMBER 22, 1963, STARTS as usual but ends a bit scary for the whole country. We have pancakes and bacon for breakfast with a glass of milk for strong bones. That's what Granny says. The bus driver gives me that same unfriendly glare I get on mornings when I am a few minutes behind Fran getting on the school bus. Jesse Adams gives me a weird look as I pass the empty seat beside him. Ever since the trip to the Austin Public Library, I have been determined to sit toward the back of the bus whenever possible. If Emma and Thomas happen to ride my bus to school, would the driver make them ride in the back? How could that ever happen in a country as great as ours? Last week, Mr. Haley had read aloud these famous words of our President, John F. Kennedy:

"The rights of every American are diminished when the rights of any group are suppressed. Our country cannot be fully free until all Americans are free because our Constitution must be colorblind."

I like those words, and I wish more people could learn to be colorblind. It sounds like President Kennedy doesn't like the idea of Black and White students having different schools, different water fountains, and separate soda fountains. These same questions are still on my mind as I look for Betty and some other girls in the lunchroom.

The loudspeaker comes on while I'm eating lunch. The announcement tells all students to return to their homerooms at 12:45. No one knows what is up. Usually at 12:45 we start fifth-period class. Why are we going to our homerooms? Maybe there will be an announcement about the students from Booker T. Washington. Betty says perhaps we will dismiss school early for Thanksgiving, but that doesn't make a bit of sense to me. As we gather up books, jackets, and anything we need for the fifth class, everyone is talking about the change, but we don't know why we have to go to homeroom.

When I enter the room, I see the look on Mr. Haley's face. He stands at the door like a soldier about to face a firing squad, and I start to worry. It's quiet in Room 106--too quiet to suit me. Even Jesse Adams is paying attention to Mr. Haley when he speaks the name of John Fitzgerald Kennedy, our President. He used to live in Washington D.C., but Mr. Kennedy doesn't live anywhere now. Someone killed him while he rode in a car in Dallas, Texas. I clench my teeth to keep back the tears and the fear those words brought to my mind. Deep in my stomach, I fear for the United States of America. If the police can't protect the President of the United States, what could happen to the rest of us?

Of course, when the time for questions comes, the boys want to know the details of the shooting. Mr. Haley tells us about the Vice-President, who hardly anyone has heard of, and how soon he will take an oath and become the new president. He tries to assure us that there is no need for alarm because the authorities have the situation under control. Every teacher in the whole wide world has those words memorized: "The situation is under control."

Mr. Haley doesn't talk about much more than that, and when Jesse asks what kind of gun the shooter has and how much blood is in the car, Mr. Haley gives him the look. He instructs us to get out our history books and says we need to study what happens in the government when we lose a president. He would allow no more blood talk. The class becomes quiet. A few of the girls cry and ask if they can see the nurse or go home. Mr. Haley lets the first two go before telling the class they should go to the back part of the schoolyard for some fresh air.

Finally, the buses arrive, and with very few words, the principal dismisses school. For the first time, Fran saves me a seat instead of sitting with her girlfriends. As each student gets off the bus, the bus driver says the exact words, "You kids stay close to each other and be safe."

Being safe and feeling safe are two different feelings. Granny sits us down on the porch swing on either side of her and holds us close as we all cry. She says she is sure that the evil person that killed President Kennedy would pay for his wicked ways. After she says a quick prayer for our safety and the safety of our country, she says we all need a break.

I sure have a lot of questions about what happened to the President. Is it possible President Kennedy's words made some people mad enough to kill him? He wanted to make the United States a better place for all citizens, Black and White. Words sure can make some people angry. Sticks and stones may break your bones, but words will never hurt you. NOT TRUE! All I want now is to feel Granny's arms around Fran and me as we sit swinging gently, back and forth, on our front porch swing.

When mom gets off work at 5:00, Granny, Fran, and I are waiting for her at the door. We go to Holt's Drugstore and have ice cream. That certainly is a pleasant way to end a sad day in Franklin, Mississippi--not only for Franklin, but for our entire country. Granny always said we should enjoy any good day because you never know what tomorrow brings. She sure was right about that. Two days later, while people watch on TV, the man who killed President Kennedy gets shot. I am glad I didn't see that because the fear that comes from the bottom of my stomach is still bothering me. This time I'm afraid even the ice cream can't help.

Elvie Clark is the only person I know who owns a TV. And yes, he saw Mr. Jack Ruby shoot Lee Harvey Oswald on national television. That's probably enough said about that, but he never tires of telling anyone with a willing ear about the details of that terrible November that changed our country.

FOURTEEN

ABOUT A MONTH LATER, our school is almost back to normal, and our principal makes another big announcement just as we settle in for our first period. The students from Booker T. Washington will be bussed to Franklin the following week. The School Board plans a town meeting to discuss this important event. The choir students will sing *The National Anthem*, and the Franklin Boy Scout Troops will carry in the flag. All parents and students are invited. I am beyond excited at the thought of getting to spend time with Emma, but my next thought is not one of excitement.

I will have to face my lies if I want to share my excitement about knowing Emma and the story of her father. I remind Granny that she has promised we will have a family meeting soon. Her promise had been months ago. No one, Granny included, seems to be ready to talk about Ted Kendrick, letters from Vietnam, or possible problems when Black students enroll at Franklin Public Schools. When I hand the note sent to all parents from the Franklin School Board to Granny at supper, I decide there is no time like the present. After Granny reads it, she passes it to Momma. Momma disagrees with the School Board's decision.

"Well, I, for one, am glad to welcome these students because I already have a friend named Emma, who is coming from Booker T. Washington."

Fran frowns at me. "Ruby Ann Kendrick, that is not the truth, and you know it. You've never been to that school, so just hush trying to sound so important."

"Fran, I don't want to hear you talking to your sister like that. Maybe Ruby can explain herself after supper when we all gather around this table for a long-overdue family meeting," Granny said.

In her quietest voice, Mom asks, "Ruby Ann, are you telling us the truth or not?"

"Yes, ma'am, I'm telling the truth."

Fran is clanging the dishes so loud, and I am clearing the table and putting the leftovers in the refrigerator. No one speaks as I wash, and Fran puts away the dishes. I am happy that soon I will be able to see Emma and find out about her father in Vietnam. Should I mention Fran's involvement in the trip to the Austin Public Library? No, no need. I plan to say that Elvie and I made the trip when I became aware of the Booker T. Washington School. Should I mention Mr. Haley? I think so. I mean, they can't ground him, that's for sure. I don't want Elvie to get into trouble either, so maybe the story of the entire trip to Austin needs to stay a secret.

As we gather around the kitchen table, Granny speaks first. "I want to begin by saying that secrets in a family can cause lots of misunderstandings, and I have been keeping a secret about Ted for too many years. I recently told June about the money Ted sends to me every month to help our family. I never told your grandfather about it because I was afraid of what he might do. I was wrong. Now, Ted is in Vietnam and making good money. He still cares about this family. From now on, whenever Ted sends a letter, this family will be told."

"If he cares about this family, then why did he leave in the first place?" Fran almost shouts her question.

No one seems ready to answer. Momma stares at the floor and looks like she has lost her best friend. The next ten seconds last an eternity. Silence.

Granny goes on. "Some matters between adults must be settled before everyone can know the answer, but Fran and Ruby deserve that answer. When Ted returns to the states, maybe he and your mother will be ready to sit down and discuss it."

"Maybe that will be possible," Tears stream down Momma's cheeks.

Granny puts her arms around her, and then looks at me.

"Now, Ruby Ann, we want to hear your secret about this friend from Booker T. Washington School."

"Mr. Haley told me about the school when he was taking some of our old books over there. He said I could ride along because he needed my help with the boxes. I told him that I had permission from home, and he believed me."

When I told one lie, it got easier to tell another.

"Anyway, Emma, that's her name. Emma Parks was on the playground crying because her daddy sent a letter from

Vietnam. He's a soldier over there just like Ted, or dad, or whoever he is. We had a good talk, but I thought I would never see her again. I'm glad she and the other kids from there are coming to Franklin Elementary, but I'm not glad that I lied about going fishing when I took off with Mr. Haley to find that school. Guess I am grounded for a while, huh?"

"Ruby Ann, why didn't you just tell us that you were going to help Mr. Haley with book boxes?"

"Well, … here goes. The whole truth is that I started walking to Booker T. Washington School, and Mr. Haley ended up giving me a ride."

"Ruby, how could you have done something so dangerous? You could have been killed walking down a busy highway."

Mom breaks down and starts crying so hard that I think she may pass out. At that point, Granny takes up the discussion and orders me to my room. Fran follows me and continues to nag me about what a crazy stunt I had pulled walking down the busiest highway in the county. When I remind her I could have told them about the bus trip to the Austin Public Library, she backs off my case. I went on to say that when that bus passed the Booker T. Washington School sign, I had decided to see that school.

"Shall I march back into the kitchen and tell mom and Granny that detail, or are you about ready to quit acting like you're my boss?"

When Fran starts crying too, I know it's time to hush. Granny and I are the only two left that aren't blubbering a bucket of tears. I find Granny and apologize with a promise never to take off like that again. She isn't crying, but the look on her face hurts me to the bottom of my heart. I deserve any punishment they decide to dish out.

"Go to your room now. Your mom and I will decide what is best to do with you," Granny says. She isn't even looking me in the eye.

Telling the whole truth about meeting Emma makes me feel better, but that good feeling doesn't last long. I am grounded for an entire month and have to miss the special meeting of the school board. In his sermons, Preacher Brewer quotes many scriptures about the virtues of being truthful. He often says the truth will set a person free. I don't feel so free sitting in my room, but at least at school, I'll get to see Emma and Thomas. Are they going to ride my bus? No, the Black students have their own bus, and they can sit anywhere they want.

Finally, the big day comes. I'm waiting outside the school door to welcome Emma and the students from Booker T. Washington School. Does everyone welcome them with open arms? No, but there aren't any National Guard soldiers here to escort the new students to Franklin Public Schools. Elvie said that in 1957, in Little Rock, Arkansas, soldiers were called in to make sure there was no violence when Black students entered a White school. Whatever happened to the idea of treating others the way you want to be treated? I know kids do crazy things sometimes, but what about adults? I mean, you can't send them to their rooms when they get downright hateful.

Elvie Clark is standing beside me as I wait on the sidewalk in front of the school. When I ask him where Jessie is, he just shrugs.

"Don't know, don't care." He has a stranger than usual look on his face.

"What are you doing out here, Ruby? The bell is gonna ring in ten minutes."

Elvie keeps looking back to the building as if something is wrong. I can tell he's worried, and I wonder if it has anything to do with Jesse. Jessie's older brothers are known as troublemakers.

Elvie pokes me in the arm. "You know that the bus from Booker T. Washington will be here any minute, right? Hey, why didn't you come to the meeting in the cafeteria about the integration of the Black students? I asked Fran where you were, and she said you were in trouble again. What's up, Ruby? You don't look so good. Here comes Mr. Dunlap. He wanted the Student Council to put up a welcome banner this morning. That didn't happen because the four officers got sick and haven't been at school all week. Strange, huh?"

"Please quit asking so many questions, Elvie. I want to see if my friend, Emma, is on the bus this morning. Seeing a familiar face might help more than any ole welcome banner."

"Why would your face be familiar to the kids on that bus? Where did you meet Emma? You're not making much sense, Ruby."

"Just stop with all the questions, and if you don't want to

welcome them, why don't you just go on into first-period class?"

"Didn't say I'm not going to welcome anyone. I'm thinking you look kinda lonely out here by yourself. Can I wait here with ya? I promise, not another question."

"It's a free country. You do what you want."

Mr. Dunlap, the principal, and five or six smiling teachers say good morning to Elvie and me. I've never seen that many adults looking so nervous. They glance down the gravel driveway as the yellow bus stops. No one speaks to the first two boys who step off the bus. They walk right past Elvie and me, and I hear Mr. Dunlap say, "Welcome." Next is a face I know. Emma stands on the top step of the bus, still holding her mother's hand. She glances back at her mom.

"She's here, Mom. I told you she would be here. Hey, Ruby, do you remember me?" Emma waves as she calls out to me.

She almost drags her mom off the bus as she looks at me. I see a tear, but I can tell from her smile she's glad to see me. A wave is all I can manage as I look at Emma. When the other six kids get off the bus, Mr. Dunlap introduces himself to Mrs. Park and the nine students who exit the bus. I hear him say that he expected more students. Mrs. Parks replies several will be coming later in the week. For once, Elvie is quiet. I'm thankful for that, along with the fact that Mrs. Parks stoops down in front of me and gives me a big hug.

"Thank you and your friend for waiting for our bus. Having kids here she knows will make this transition go smoother for Emma and her brother too. I'm Brenda Parks, and this is my son, Thomas. You already know Emma. I understand you two met this summer. I'm looking forward to seeing Mr. Haley again, too. Please introduce me to your friend here."

For a moment, I can't think of anyone to introduce except Elvie. A friend? Well, I suppose at times, like this morning, he might be called a friend. He has helped me keep some secrets along the way. I certainly will be in a lot more trouble if Elvie decides to spill the beans about the Austin bus trip.

"This is Elvie Clark, and he'll be in the same grade with Emma and me."

The look on Elvie's face is priceless. Being true to his word, he doesn't ask one question. Just a nod. He stares at me and darts his eyes back and forth between Emma and me.

"I'm so glad you could be here to welcome us this morning, Elvie. You and Ruby are outstanding ambassadors for your school. With your principal and teachers, you've helped make this day go smoothly at our new school," said Mrs. Parks.

Mr. Dunlap steps forward to introduce everyone there. The other students stare at the ground and hug a notebook to their chests, like a shield protecting them from a charging army.

Mrs. Parks introduces Emma and Thomas first, then the others, and tells Mr. Dunlap what grade the students will be entering. The bell rings, so Mr. Dunlap tells Mrs. Parks and the other students to follow him to the cafeteria for an orientation. When he says Elvie and I will also be included as school ambassadors, I almost faint. Elvie has this stupid grin on his face that I've seen many times, when he is trying to impress someone with his knowledge. I meet Thomas and learn that he will be in the eighth grade, the same grade as Fran. At least he will not be the only black student in that grade because he has a friend named Joe who stays close by his side. Thomas and Joe, well, how shall I say this? They have a look like they are ready to turn and run any minute.

I can hear Granny's voice in my head, "Just give it some time." When I try to introduce Elvie and myself to Joe and Thomas, I reach out to shake hands, but they don't take their hands out of their pockets. Not a word is spoken, so there is nothing to do but take a deep breath and move on.

"Never mind my brother and Joe, they think they are too big to listen to anyone. But Momma laid down the law this morning before the bus left our old school. Mr. Haley will talk to my mom every day to make sure this new school business goes smooth. If anyone gets a bad report, our daddy will take care of it when he gets home. Ruby, do ya know my momma is going to work in the lunchroom here? That's another reason Thomas is bein' so stubborn. He wasn't happy when she took the job, 'cause he thinks she doesn't trust us to behave. Could be. Anyway, I was so glad to see your face when I got off the bus. I almost started to cry, but I remembered you don't like crybabies."

Mr. Dunlap takes the other students to their classrooms, leaving Emma, Elvie, and me. I have to say I am proud of

Elvie for not asking a million questions, but when Emma mentions that she has a letter from her dad in Vietnam, the silence ends.

"My name is Elvie Clark, and I have a TV at my house. You are welcome to come anytime and see the news about Vietnam. Is your dad a pilot? When I get out of school, I'm gonna train to be a helicopter pilot and rescue wounded soldiers in Vietnam. When did you come to Franklin and meet Ruby? We did a report on Vietnam last year...."

I'm glad Mr. Dunlap interrupts Elvie at that point. I sure don't want her to think that Elvie and I are best friends. Now it's time for third-hour classes, so off we go to find Mr. Haley's history class. Emma sits next to me, and Elvie is on the opposite side of the room. Thank goodness for small favors. Periods three and four go by quickly, and then lunchtime comes. The noise level in the lunchroom is different. The room hasn't been this quiet since the day President Kennedy was shot. Emma, Elvie, and I sit where all the fourth graders are assigned. I believe every eye is on us as we sit down to eat.

Jesse Adams and Betty Mangrum usually sit close to us, but today they skip ten spaces and give us a look like we are contagious. Mr. Haley and Mr. Dunlap come over and make everyone scoot over closer, and Emma's momma comes out of the kitchen just long enough to kiss Emma on the head. Mr. Haley sits on one side of Emma, and I am on the other. Soon the conversation is back to normal, almost. The fifth graders and the other students are allowed to sit anywhere they want, and I notice that Thomas and the other Black students all sit together at the end of a table nearest to the entry door. So, this is the type of welcome that Franklin Public Schools gives the Booker T. Washington students. At the very least, we don't have to call in the National Guard today.

FIFTEEN

MR. HALEY AND THE other teachers do all they can to keep the school running smoothly. Not much changes for the rest of the school year. Mr. Haley works tirelessly to keep our history class informed of world events. When he asks the class what we know about a man named Dr. Martin Luther King Jr., Elvie is the first to answer.

"He is a Baptist preacher, and I heard part of his famous speech that he made in Washington DC. He travels all over the country speaking about equal rights for all Americans."

Not wanting to be outdone, Jesse Adams decides to share what he knows. "Since he is a Junior, he has the same name as his father."

This remark gets a big laugh from the class, but Mr. Haley doesn't look too happy.

"You are right, Jessie. His father is also named Martin Luther King. Maybe tomorrow you can tell us more about this famous person and his family."

Jessie sticks his bottom lip out in the most giant pout ever. I'll bet he wishes he could take back his little joke.

Mr. Haley goes on making assignments. "Elvie, will you tell the class more about Mr. King's famous speech?" The project is undoubtedly a challenge to Elvie, who begins to use the index to his history book to gather facts.

"I want all of you to choose a topic off my list of current events to make a report to share with the class next week." Mr. Haley has selected thirty topics for us to choose from for our report. After five minutes to look over the list, everyone has to pick five that sound interesting.

"Mr. Haley, if I don't like any of these subjects, can I choose my own?" Roy Mason asked. Snickering springs up across the room. Mr. Haley looks over the top of his glasses at Roy. We all know the answer to Roy's question is a definite 'no.'

"Y'all choose five off the list, and I will make the final selection and tell you the next day what your assignment will be." He begins to erase the board as the bell rings.

Emma tells me she wants to write about Martin Luther King Jr. or the Vietnam War. Those are my choices, too.

Jesse Adams raises his hand. "Can I write about the Ku Klux Klan?"

"Jesse, I asked you to choose off the list. That topic isn't on my list."

"But that ain't fair 'cause Elvie got his choice."

"Jesse, Elvie's topic is on the list, but if you want to talk about more, we will discuss it further after school."

"I can't stay after school. My daddy will get mad, 'cause I got chores to do at home." Jesse pouted again.

"Jesse, if you think I'm unfair, we can go down and talk to the principal." All of a sudden, Jesse finds another topic.

If I get Vietnam, I can use the letters from Ted and get information about the war. After class, I managed to catch up with Emma. "Emma, ask your mom if you can spend Friday night with me. We can work on our reports together. I'll talk to mom as soon as I get home if ya want to come."

"I would like to come, and if we can work together on school reports, my mom will probably agree."

When I ask Momma, she says she needs to talk to Emma's mom before I can have overnight company. I tell her Mrs. Parks works in the school cafeteria, so my mother goes to school early the following day to meet her.

Granny says that some people are prejudiced against people of a different color. I told her that is their problem, not mine. Prejudice is one of our vocabulary words in reading class, but I didn't think it is why Jesse and Betty decided not to be my friend anymore. I already know about separate bus seats and drinking fountains. Anyway, Momma says Mrs. Parks is nice, and she would love to let Emma spend some Friday night at our house. I wonder if Emma can sit on the school bus in the front with me. Who should I ask? Mr. Dunlap? The bus driver? Mr. Haley? All of a sudden, this thing prejudice is my problem. I will ask Granny. She will know what I need to do.

"Granny, I have an important question to ask you about my sleepover with Emma. Momma says she can spend next Friday night with me, but how are we gonna get home from school?"

"The same way you get home from school every day, on

the bus. Is that a problem?"

"I suppose not, but Emma says that when her family takes a bus to Austin, the bus driver always makes them sit in the back, and the White people sit in the front. If we can't sit together, then we'll just walk home."

"Gracious, child! These kids from Booker T. Washington are now at Franklin Elementary Public School, so y'all get treated the same. Don't go looking for trouble, girl. If there are any problems about your friend spending the night, you just let Mr. Dunlap know."

When I tell mom and Granny that I plan to write a report on Vietnam in history class, mom looks worried. They don't say anything, but Granny and Mom exchange looks. Maybe Vietnam isn't such a good topic after all. Adults! You can never tell what they are thinking. Oh, well, Vietnam will be my choice unless Mr. Haley decides differently.

Before bedtime, Mom comes to our room to talk to Fran and me about Ted. In her hand, she holds a letter that had come that day. She wants to read it to us. The letter starts with 'Dear Family.' Now he remembers he has a family? I have to tell myself to focus and not be so negative, but this is a lot to think about. Fran and I both listen quietly and say nothing when she finishes. She asks if we have any questions. I shake my head, and Fran whispers 'no.' In the letter, Ted says that he's looking forward to coming home. He adds that he hopes to be back in the states after Christmas. The letter closes by saying, "Sincerely Yours, Ted." If he had written *Love Always*, I think I probably would have thrown up my supper for sure.

That doesn't exactly sound like a person who has been a stranger for ten years. Sending money is one thing, but having Ted living with us is a big step for sure.

"Are you sure you don't want to ask me any questions about your dad? What do you think about him coming here after Christmas?" Mom quietly folded the letter and put it in her apron pocket.

There were no words to express the thoughts swirling in my head. Fran just stares at the floor. Fran and I both just shake our heads five or six times, then Fran says, "Good night, Mom."

After our mother turns the light off and closes the door, I hear Fran crying.

"Why do you suppose Ted is thinking about coming home now?" I just have to ask.

After blowing her nose ten times, Fran finally gets up from her bed and comes over to sit on my side of the bed. "Maybe, it's because Granny told him how worried we are about you."

"Me? Who is worried about me? His coming back here has nothing to do with me. That's the craziest thing I ever heard you say."

"Yea, well, Momma and Granny have been frettin' ever since you told them you took off walking to that Booker T. Washington School. They think you are going to run off or something. Now, you want to learn more about Vietnam. They probably think you're going take off to Memphis and try to fly to Vietnam. Ruby, you are so unpredictable. Why can't you just leave well enough alone? Forget it. I'm sorry that I said anything."

"Well, you should be sorry." After a moment's pause, I asked, "Fran, are you glad Ted might be coming home?"

"I don't know how I feel now, but I think having a dad at home like most of the other kids might be a good thing. Don't you think so?"

"I've changed my mind. THAT is the craziest thing you have ever said. Good night. Go to sleep. No more talking."

No more talking doesn't stop the ideas from floating around in my brain. How can Fran think that a stranger moving into this house will be a good thing? How can anyone let ten years pass and think money will buy him a welcome back into our family? One thing is for sure. I will never welcome him back, no matter what Mom or Granny has to say. I lay awake for hours, trying to make sense of what's happening in my world. But Christmas is a long way off. A lot can happen in six weeks.

SIXTEEN

BEFORE I KNOW IT, Friday finally arrives. Emma and I have plans for a fun sleepover. When Betty Mangrum overhears our conversation in the lunchroom, she sticks her tongue out at us and goes to put her tray up without eating a bite. Some people! When the bell rings at the end of the day, Emma gets her bag and schoolbooks, and we start out the door. I feel many eyes looking our way. Emma doesn't seem a bit nervous, so I just shrug off the uneasy feeling.

The bus driver has to help the younger kids find their assigned seats, so he isn't in his seat when I notice Jesse Adams blocking the bus door. He shakes his fist right in Emma's face and tells her and me that we have to walk home.

"What makes you think you are the boss of this bus, anyway?" I stare him right in the face and shake my fist at him.

"We can go to the lunchroom and ride with my mom," said Emma. She looks like she's going to cry and begins to back away. That's when she bumps into Elvie, who has never ridden a school bus in his whole life. What in the world is he doing in the bus rider line? Suddenly, he squeezes right between Jesse and me. He drags Jesse out of the doorway of the bus. I grab Emma by the hand, and we go up the steps and straight to my assigned seat. I glance out the window and see the bus driver, Jesse, and Elvie having a serious talk. The other kids all stand up and stare. The bus driver shouts that we all better sit down.

Elvie takes off running and returns in a few minutes with Mr. Dunlap right behind him.

This is the first time I have ever seen the principal on a bus. He escorts Jesse to his seat and tells us all to have a good weekend. Elvie waves at us as the bus pulls out in line. Emma and I both waved back. I just hope whatever Mr. Dunlap has to say to Jesse and his brothers will scare them into leaving us alone. I'm not so sure I want to know what's about to happened. I am glad that Jesse and his brothers and sisters sit behind us. We can get off the bus without having to pass them. As we get closer to my house, I try to talk to Emma, but she still looks scared. As the bus slows to stop at the end of the lane leading to my house, I take Emma's hand and tell her this is my stop. We walk down the aisle and steps, and I tell Emma everything is okay. She smiles, and I tell her about Granny's sugar cookies. Then we hear someone yell from the bus.

"Your kind doesn't belong on our bus."

The next thing I know, Emma screams and grabs her overnight bag to her chest. Someone on the bus has thrown something that flew right past my head. Another object hits Emma's bag, so we both run as fast as we can down the lane. We run until we get to the steps where Mom and Granny meet us. They look almost as scared as we do. Red tomato juice and seeds are dripping down the overnight bag, and Emma's dress is wet with the same sticky mess.

"Lands, child, what did you two girls get into?" Granny is shaking as hard as I am. "You look like the devil himself is chasing you."

"Somebody threw tomatoes at us when we got off the bus. It wasn't the devil on our bus. It was Jesse Adams."

After several minutes of questioning from Mom and Granny, Fran came rushing down the road. "The bus driver thinks it was one of the Adams boys that yelled out the window. He got them by the collar and told them to sit on the bus steps. He flagged down a car. Someone will get the word to Mr. Dunlap soon."

"Did you see Jesse throw the tomatoes?" asks Momma.

"No, but I know his voice. When we started to get on the bus, he talked mean to Emma and me. He blocked the door until Elvie showed up and pulled him out of the way." Granny looks up when she hears Elvie's name.

"You mean Elvie was there when you girls were getting on the bus? What was he doing there? Did he talk to the bus driver?"

About that time, Granny turns toward the house and throws up her hands. We all could smell something burning.

"The cookies are burning," yelled Granny as we ran up the steps.

We raise every window in the house, decide to sit on the porch, and wait for the school principal to show up, all except Emma. She goes in to change her clothes and wipe her backpack off.

I tell Granny to call as soon as Mr. Dunlap shows up, and I go in to help Emma. I don't want to miss any of the discussion with the principal. If Jesse happens to be with Mr. Dunlap, I have a few words to say to him, too. It isn't long before we are all sitting around the kitchen table with Mr. Dunlap.

"Now, I want Emma to tell me what happened when you girls started to board the bus this afternoon. Take your time, and if you don't know the names of those involved, just describe what they were wearing. Okay? Can you do that, Emma?"

Emma nods. "When Ruby and I started toward the bus, we saw a boy in a blue shirt standing in front of the bus door. He let several kids get on with no problem, but he blocked the door when it was our turn to go up the steps. When he didn't move, I didn't say a word. I started to back up and bumped into Elvie Clark. He always saves Ruby and me a seat in the lunchroom, so I'm not afraid of him. He said something to the boy. Elvie grabbed him by the elbow and pulled him out of our way. Then we got on the bus, and I looked at the floor the whole time until it was time to get off."

"I heard a voice that yelled at us, and I know who...."

"Now, Ruby, just let Emma finish. I promise you will get to tell us later any details Emma might not recall," adds Mr. Dunlap.

"Sorry, I didn't mean to interrupt. It just happens a lot."

"I understand, Ruby. Emma is very fortunate to have you as a friend."

Mr. Dunlap sure knows how to make kids feel good. No one has ever said that having me as a friend makes them fortunate. Usually, when I interrupt an adult, I end up spending some quiet time alone in my bedroom. Now I am fortunate for my friends. As it all ends this afternoon, I get to tell the most exciting part about flying objects and even what they yelled at us from the bus. Emma says she isn't for sure what they said, but I believe she just wants to let me talk for a while.

Mr. Dunlap tells us the Adams boys will not be allowed back on the bus until after Christmas. A teacher will sit on the bus with them for a while to make sure they have learned their lesson. A glass of cold milk and Granny's cookies right out of the oven sure can make the world seem better.

Emma and I sit on the front porch swing for a while. I hope that trouble on the bus doesn't make her not want to come back to my house.

"Your family sure does make me feel welcome. When your mom came by the lunchroom to see my mom, she knew everything would be fine. Tell me about your dad. Is he getting to come home soon?"

"It's a complicated story about my dad. His name is Ted, but I don't really know much about him. He left my family before I could even talk, and Mom cried so much. It was much easier when no one mentioned him. So, he is a stranger to me. Fran says she can remember him because she was almost four years old when something happened between him and my mom. I really don't want to talk about him anymore."

I sit on the swing beside Emma for several minutes with my head in my hands. I can't believe the words that came out of my mouth. They just slipped out. I promised myself to face the truth long ago and never refuse to talk about something even if it isn't pleasant. For more than ten years, Mom hasn't wanted to talk about Ted. Now I am doing to Emma what my mom has done to me. I lift my head and tell Emma that I will try to explain about my dad sometime, but not now.

I want this weekend to be fun, even though it has already gotten off on a sour note. Fran promises she will play hide-and-seek with us after supper, and I have to show Emma my super best hiding places before Fran sees us take off into the backyard. Granny and Mom have already taken the Chinese Checker game out. Mom's frying chicken for supper. Ted Kendrick is not going to ruin another minute of our sleepover.

While we are still sitting at the table eating supper, we hear a knock at the door. Mom goes to the door and escorts Elvie Clark and his mom into the kitchen.

"Please, sit down at the table with us," said Granny. "We were about to have some homemade apple pie. Won't you let us share our supper with you?"

"No, no, we have already eaten," said Mrs. Clark.

Elvie frowns. "Well, we didn't have any homemade apple pie with our supper." He is eyeing Granny's pie like he hasn't eaten in a month. "Please, Mom, I want to tell Ruby and Emma what happened at lunch today."

"I suppose we could sit down for a while and let the children talk," replies Mrs. Clark.

"Fine," said Granny. "Sit here while I get some plates for the apple pie."

"None for me, thank you," said Mrs. Clark.

"Yes, ma'am, a big slice, please." Elvie always smiles a mile when food is coming.

Between bites, Elvie tells his account of what he saw in the lunchroom. He noticed something red on the floor when he went over to pick up his backpack. When he realized it was a tomato and that Toby, big brother of Jesse Adams, quickly picked it up, he got suspicious. He waited until Toby's friends gathered around and started to laugh. The last part of the conversation was about teaching that black girl a lesson. There are only six black girls at Franklin School, and Elvie knew Emma was having a sleepover at Ruby's house.

"Ruby, I'm sorry I didn't go straight to the office at noon to tell the principal about the tomato, but I didn't want to be late for class. "

"Elvie, you don't need to apologize to anyone. You have helped many times since we had to change schools. Thomas and I have felt welcome, mainly because of you and Ruby." Emma finishes with a beautiful smile.

"Oh, it's nothing, really. I just want those Adams boys to know that they better be careful who they are messing with," said Elvie.

I bite my tongue not to say something about Elvie being so tough. I know this isn't the time to bring up the outcome of our last wrestling match. Somehow that seems like a long time ago. Finally, Mrs. Clark announces that she and Elvie have to go.

After several games of Chinese Checkers, I remind Fran that she promised us a game of hide and seek in the backyard. I feel good to be hiding and giggling quietly with Emma. Fran searches for more than fifteen minutes before she finds us. Then she decides to hide with Emma while I do the looking. Fran is laughing and running around as I haven't seen her do for a long while. Next, Granny asks us to find her some lightning bugs and put them in a jar because she and Popaw used to do that together when they were younger. Emma is good at catching lightning bugs, and she isn't a bit afraid to let the bugs crawl right up to her elbow. That is just another reason I know Emma and I are gonna have a friendship that will last.

Later, we all sit around the table and play Go Fish with a deck of cards and drink hot chocolate until Granny announces time for bed. It's been an almost perfect day, even if it did start out a bit scary on the bus. Saturday morning, we decided it was time to get busy on report outlines. Because Emma wants Vietnam, I am going to write about John F. Kennedy.

We have other sleepovers before Christmas break. Emma and I get a chance to talk about our families. Thomas always wants to read aloud the letters their father sends from Vietnam. I get such a lump in my throat every time Emma mentions her father. Finally, Emma quits asking any questions about Ted. I know being angry at someone I don't remember doesn't make a bit of sense, but those feelings don't go away easily. It's true I didn't know him, but I can see what his absence has done to my family. Preacher Brewer has preached the last three Sundays in a row about forgiveness. Each week he looks straight at me.

Our reports for Mr. Haley's history class are due the Friday before Christmas break. Elvie never misses a chance to remind us he has a television if we want to come by and get the latest news about current events. He and his mom have planned a trip to the library in Austin to listen to Martin Luther King's speech called "I Have a Dream." Mrs. Clark has made a point to invite Emma and me to go over to the Austin Public Library with them on Saturday before school is out for Christmas. I am glad that Emma's mom wouldn't let her go along because of her Saturday chores. I'm not happy she has all those chores, but that gives me a good excuse not to go. I'll say my family needs me at home to help Granny cut up the last of the garden's cucumbers for pickles. No one needs to know I volunteered for that chore. There's no way I want to travel in a car to Austin with just Elvie and his mom.

Anyway, I've been thinking about the other trip to the Austin Public Library and those signs saying, "Whites Only" or, "No Colored People Allowed." How would Emma feel if she saw those signs? If I ever saw a sign posted that said, "No Whites Allowed," I would probably just march into that place and give the owner a piece of my mind, but not Emma. She is fun-loving and giggly as I am when we are by ourselves. But, at school, she is so quiet and looks down at the floor a lot. I tell her she will bump into the wall if she doesn't start looking up more. She smiles and says okay, but she never changes.

Preacher Brewer's favorite scripture is all about learning to get along with other people. He says blessed are the peacemakers. I have no hope of ever being called a peacemaker, but Emma probably will win that title someday. I feel pretty blessed to have a friend like Emma.

On Monday of the last week of school before Christmas break, I've written only one paragraph about John Fitzgerald Kennedy. Mr. Haley says I should mention his years in the Navy, his Purple Heart Medal, and the Cold War. He also suggests I should only include one short paragraph on how he died. I decide the Purple Heart Medal is more important than any cold weather problems. I don't know anything about a cold war. I am more interested in Vietnam, but that's Emma's report. She mentions letters from her dad and all the places where he has been stationed in Vietnam. Mr. Haley asks how many other students know a soldier serving in Vietnam. I don't raise my hand.

Finally, Elvie has his turn and tells everyone about Martin Luther King Jr. and his famous speech. I try to listen, but I can't see what is so important about a dream of going to the top of a mountain. Does Elvie even mention where this mountain is located? I don't think so. I am not about to ask him.

SEVENTEEN

TWO WHOLE WEEKS AND no school. No homework. That also means two weeks full-time with my sister. Granny tries her best to keep us busy making Christmas cards for the family and doing some extra baking to share with our neighbors. The most fun event of the first week off is stringing popcorn. Emma, Thomas, and Mrs. Parks come over on Friday afternoon, and Momma pops three pans of popcorn. We sit in the living room with our needles and thread and eat as much popcorn as we want. Eventually, we're full of popcorn and start making strings for the tree, all except Thomas. Granny thinks he may have a holler leg 'cause he is still eating popcorn and drinking Kool-Aid. He downs four glasses while everyone else is putting popcorn strings on our tree.

Mrs. Parks invites us over the next day to put popcorn strings on their tree. She also says that her husband will be discharged from the Army the following week. He might be home before January. I have never seen Thomas smile as big as when he starts to talk about his daddy coming home. He talks about hunting, fishing, and planting a larger garden when his mouth isn't full of popcorn. Emma is quieter than usual, and I catch her looking at me with a sideways look.

After Mrs. Parks' big announcement, Mom has news to tell too. "I have heard from my husband, too. He hopes to be here for Christmas. He has been away for a long time, even before Vietnam. Mrs. Parks, I hope both of our families are blessed with safe returns from this terrible war."

Emma replies, "I can't wait for my daddy to meet my new friends at school. Mr. Haley says my daddy can wear his uniform and show the class on the map where he was in Vietnam.

Her momma frowns. "Well, now, Emma, you will need to take that invitation up with your daddy when he gets home. You gather up these popcorn strings that the Kendricks have helped us make. Tomorrow afternoon, we will decorate some pinecones and make wreaths for our house. Having neighbors to share in the fun of Christmas sure has been something special. We're going to make some peanut candy too. Hope to see y'all tomorrow. Does three o'clock in the afternoon sound okay?"

"That is just fine with us. I can't remember the last time we've had company over for the holidays." Mom's smile lit up her face. It certainly has been a while since that happened.

"The girls and I will bring some Christmas cookies too."

After all the good nights and thanks are said, our house seems too quiet. Granny has the biggest grin on her face I have seen since Popaw passed. Mom is offering to go over to Emma's and bring cookies. Would wonders never cease? What kind of changes will come to our house when Ted--if

Ted—comes back from the war? If he expects me to welcome him back with open arms, he has another think coming. Christmas cheer can only go so far when it comes to Ted Kendrick. No matter what Fran, Mom, or Granny say, time doesn't heal all wounds. And yes, I feel wounded.

It's hard to pout when everyone around you is happy with holiday cheer. So I decide not to think about *him* until *he* comes through the door. In one more week, we will have presents to open and time to sleep late. Granny announces we have to do some serious cleaning from room to room. She plans to bake special pies and cakes and even shop for new shoes. I start to object to the shopping trip for new shoes. My tennis shoes are kinda scuffed, but a good scrubbing will take care of that. Oh well, having two pairs of shoes that fit will be a new experience for me.

Preacher Brewer and his family come over the Sunday before Christmas, and Granny tells me to be on my best behavior. Fried chicken, creamed potatoes with brown gravy, peas, corn, and pecan pie for dessert make up our Sunday dinner. I sure hope Mom and Granny saved enough good food for Christmas Eve dinner. Emma's family is coming so we can go out to sing Christmas carols. After that, we'll have hot chocolate and cookies, too. Every time we hear someone knock on the door, I have a knot in my stomach. I'm not about to ask, but I want to know if Mom has gotten any word from Ted. Fran says she doesn't know, and all Granny would say is go and ask your mom.

I might get up the nerve to ask Mom about those ten years

that are still a mystery. Granny knows details, but she won't talk about it. If Popaw were still alive, I know he would just lay it all out on the table. Maybe Fran is right when she tells me to let some questions go unanswered. But that doesn't make a lick of sense to me. Soon there would be more important matters to talk about.

Christmas comes and Christmas goes. No Ted. School will start back in four days. I'm sitting around thinking about the past. I'm about to go crazy, thinking about stuff that no one wants to talk about.

"I would like to ask some questions, Granny. Before you say, ask your mom, I want to know why you won't tell me the truth about all those Vietnam letters from Ted."

Granny has just started to stir up some cornbread in front of the oven. She looks up at me sitting at the kitchen table. First, she takes her apron off and wipes her hands. Then she turns around and turns off the oven. She is serious.

"Well, Ruby, I reckon you deserve some answers, but since your mom is over at Mrs. Clark's, we can't have a family meeting now. After supper, the four of us can have a more detailed talk if your mom agrees. Okay, shoot me a few questions, and I will be as honest as I can."

It's my turn to talk, and I just can't seem to decide how to get the words out. What if Ted and Popaw got into a big fight and the police made him leave? What if Ted did something wrong and had to leave town on the run? What if he left because he hadn't wanted another girl, ME, in his family? In Bible days, it seems like the fathers always wanted sons. What if he just can't stand the thought of not having a son?

"Is it my fault that Ted left?" I blurt out.

"Gracious, child! You were still in diapers. Where did you get that notion?" Granny comes over to the table, sits next to me, and pulls me into her lap. It doesn't matter that my feet are dragging on the floor. Her arms around me and my head on her shoulder feel good. The smell of Dove soap and cornmeal makes me feel safe and warm. I'm determined not to start crying, so I sit there thinking hard about my next question. When I finally get my words together, I sit up straight and decide to say it straight.

"Most men, at least in Bible days, always want a son. Was Ted so disappointed that I wasn't a boy?"

"Oh my, Ruby Ann. You do have an imagination. Your daddy loved you so much when you were born. He barely let me and your Popaw hold you any. When your mom was still too weak to go to church, Ted helped us get you and Fran ready for church. Sometimes I thought he only went to church to show you two girls off. Please believe me. Ted's leaving has nothing to do with you or Fran. Now, you know all the years he's been gone, he sent back part of his paycheck to help us out. I was afraid that your Popaw wouldn't accept his money, so I never told him. I guess I was wrong to do that. But that's water under the bridge now. Things were not always good for Ted and your mom."

"You mean that Mom is the reason that Ted left? She made him?"

"I didn't say that. Everyone makes mistakes. Forgiving

yourself and others is not easy. It's like a fight going on inside your mind. It takes time to work it all out. Please don't ever think your parents splitting up has anything to do with you or your sister. Usually, kids do better than most adults when it comes to fighting this battle of forgiveness,"

"So, you think Mom and Ted or whatever he wants to be called--do you think they are ready to forgive and forget? "

"It does look that way. Do you think you can forgive and forget?"

"Maybe, but I am still not sure what it is I am supposed to forget. If you and Mom can do it, I reckon I can too. What's for supper, Granny? My stomach is starting to growl, and I really need some food."

"Well, get out of the kitchen. Go and see if you can find us some eggs so I can finish the cornbread. We're having peas, turnip greens, and stewed potatoes to go with our cornbread. I might have time to make bread pudding if you take off now and get those eggs gathered."

After gathering eleven eggs and putting them in the kitchen sink, I run to find Fran. She has her nose in a book as usual. When I tell her about the family meeting after supper, I finally get her attention.

"Ruby, why does Granny think we need to have a family meeting? What have you done now?"

"Not a thing, except tell Granny that we deserve some answers about Ted coming home."

"Wow! All of a sudden, you have something to say about our dad living here."

"If you are going to start acting like Miss Smarty Pants, I'm not saying another word."

"Okay, sorry. What kind of questions are you going to ask?"

"I am going to ask Mom why Ted left and did she make him leave."

"Ruby, please don't do that. Mom will be so upset, and you know she'll start crying. Why can't you leave well enough alone?"

"What in the world does well enough mean? Granny kept secrets for ten years about Ted. Mom cries every time his name comes up, and you want to welcome him back with open arms. If that is what well enough is supposed to be, I don't want no part of it."

"Just remember that everything in this life is not always black and white. Asking a lot of questions about the past could make matters worse. Maybe you should just forget about the past and make the most of what is about to happen." Fran's voice was stern. "Don't ask Mom about that part of her past. Back then she was so sad that she'd go days and not come out of her room. I remember those days, don't you? Is that what you want again? You might not want any part of what 'well enough sounds like,' but maybe, it will be better than before. Don't ask a million questions, please, Ruby. Don't make everything worse by bringing up the past."

I decide to write out a few questions and show them to Granny before I get up my nerve to talk to Mom. As I sit on my bed with paper and pencil, I hear the screen door open and then shut. Mom is home. But what she tells us, even before we sit down to eat supper, makes me forget all about my questions.

Momma tells us that Mrs. Clark had a phone call from a friend from Jackson, Mississippi, to inform her about a bus wreck. This friend works as a nurse, and she knows that some who were injured had been traveling to Franklin. Two of the hospitalized were soldiers. They had been discharged from the Army and had been in Vietnam. No names were released, but Mrs. Clark knew that Ted Kendrick and James Parks were supposed to be home around the holidays. Mom isn't crying, but she is as white as a sheet. Her voice was calm when she spoke to Granny.

"If you and the girls will be okay here, Mrs. Clark and I are going to ride over to talk with the Parks family. Brenda Parks and I will try to call the hospital from the Clark's house. Then we'll decide what our next step needs to be. You girls, help Granny with supper. As soon as we know anything, I'll be back home."

Just like that, my questions are stuffed into my pants pocket. Mom is back out the door, and Granny says, "It's time for us to say a prayer for our food and the safety of our friends and family."

I am not near as hungry as I had been just thirty minutes earlier. Each mouthful just seems to form a ball in my throat, and it won't go down. No one talks after the prayer. The only sound I hear is water dripping in the kitchen sink and the ticking of the clock that hangs in the living room. It's Granny's

Cuckoo clock that had been handed down for over three generations in the Smith family. When the hour strikes seven and the little Cuckoo bird comes out to call the hour, we all freeze.

"That is one sound I can do without right now." Granny silences the sounding bird.

If Emma had been here, she would have been counting aloud each time the bird made his call. I wonder what Emma and Thomas are doing right now. They must be home alone, waiting for their mom to return. Hopefully, she isn't crying. I am sure glad Fran and I aren't alone. Fran gets up and tries to stop the dripping sound of the water in the sink, but it isn't any use. That is just one more job that seems to go undone after Popaw passed away.

"Come on, girls. We have dishes to wash and put away. We can keep our hands busy, and maybe that will help keep the wrong thoughts out of our minds. Your mom will be back before long. Then we will know what tomorrow is going to bring," Granny tells us.

When we finally go to our rooms at midnight, hoping to sleep, no one talks. Fran and I just lay down with our clothes on and fall asleep from exhaustion. As the sun starts to peek through the window shades, I sit up suddenly when I hear Mom's voice. I run to the kitchen to find Granny and Mom drinking their coffee. They look like neither one of them has slept a wink.

"Good morning, baby girl, come sit down and I'll get you a glass of milk. First, go get your sister up because I will be leaving for the hospital in Jackson in a couple of hours."

"Who is in the hospital? What about Emma's dad?" I ask.

"Please go get your sister, and I promise to answer all of your questions and tell y'all what I know now."

Fran is already brushing her hair and getting ready to put on clean clothes when I tell her Mom is home. She looks at me and starts to cry. Suddenly, I put my arms around her waist and tell her there is nothing to cry about. I tell her that Mom wants to talk to us before she goes to the hospital. I give her a big hug.

"This is good news because at least someone in the hospital isn't dead."

"You're right, little sister. You do have a way with words."

After she dries her tears, Fran and I go into the kitchen. I wonder what Mom and Mrs. Parks have found out about the bus wreck in Jackson. Mom looks tired, but she seems to be calm as she tells us what she has learned. Both Ted and Mr. Parks have survived the wreck. Both have several injuries, but they should heal before long. Mom and Mrs. Parks have decided to make the trip to the hospital.

"Mrs. Clark has been such a help in getting all our plans together. We decided we would take the bus because not knowing the area could be a real problem. She told us of her cousin who lives in Jackson. After a few calls, her cousin agreed to meet us at the bus station and get us to the hospital."

Granny hugs mom and says, "Well, bless her soul! Whatever would we do without our friends?"

"I need to get some things together for the trip. The bus leaves at 2:00. You girls be good for Granny and pray that we have a safe trip to the hospital and back home before long."

EIGHTEEN

EMMA, THOMAS, FRAN, GRANNY, and I spend the next few days playing cards, taking walks, and getting to know each other a whole lot better. And, oh yes, Elvie shows up on our front porch every single day. Granny reminds us that his mother has been nice enough to offer Mom and Mrs. Parks a place to stay close to the hospital, so we should always include Elvie in our plans. Eventually, Thomas and Elvie leave us three girls alone, so it's easy to forget that Elvie thinks he knows everything about everything.

Ted was injured the worst in the bus crash. He has a broken leg and several facial cuts that require stitches. Mr. Parks has no broken bones but still has some internal injuries that require many tests. Mom and Mrs. Parks are staying with Elvie's Aunt June in Jackson for a few days before catching the bus back to Franklin.

Granny stays busy keeping us all fed and going back and forth between our house and the Park's house. Who would have ever thought having pigs to care for would take so much time? Every other day we take corn out to the pen and make sure they have plenty of water. Thank goodness, the hog pen is quite a distance behind the house because when the wind blows out of the north, that pig pen is enough to gag us all. Give me chickens any day because pigs simply aren't worth the trouble. Thomas disagrees with me about pigs. He tells us the price of pork is going up and that their profits will grow every year. I will have to give credit to Elvie. When it's time to feed and water the animals, he's right here doing his part.

Finally, Granny hears from the hospital. Mom and Mrs. Parks will be home on Monday, and both patients will be released the following week. The Army has arranged a ride home by van for Ted and Mr. Parks. We get busy. We plan a coming-home party at the school gym for the following Tuesday afternoon. The whole town is invited. Granny makes gallons of Kool-Aid punch, and Mrs. Clark provides cookies in the shape of the American flag with delicious red, white, and blue icing. Everyone is so excited and happy. That is everyone, except me.

I may be nervous, uncertain, and a little bit proud, but I'm not excited or happy. I've not had the chance to talk with Granny about why Ted left in the first place. Fran won't talk to me about how our life is about to change. She says let the past stay in the past and stomps off with her nose in the air. The best thing for me to do is wait. Everyone knows I'm not good at waiting. While Granny is stirring Kool-Aid, I give her a big hug and whisper, "You owe me a family meeting. I will try to be patient for a little while."

≈

Elvie finds a recording of the National Anthem to play on his record player. He starts the music as the van stops in front of the gym. The crowds outside are waiting with their hands on their hearts. Mr. Parks gets out first. Thomas and his mom are there to help support him. Emma grabs him around the waist when he almost loses his balance. Everyone cheers as the family of four walks down the sidewalk. My dad — okay, I said it — my dad is next, and because of his crutches, he has to move pretty slow. Mom gives him the first hug and kiss. She and Fran stand beside him as he waves to many friends he has known over the years. He stoops down to eye level as Granny and I move in his direction. I put out my hand to shake hands, but he pulls me to him and kisses me, not Fran, but me, on the cheek. Fran does get a hug and kiss, but mine came first.

Why did I lose all my words? I feel small. Mom and Granny's mouths are moving, but I've lost their words, too. I hear Elvie's record player, but everything else is a blur. Granny grabs my hand, and the five of us walk slowly into the gym. I hear people clapping their hands and Mayor Jones on the speaker asking everyone to sit down for introductions. The high school choir sings *America the Beautiful*. Then we all put our hands on our hearts while we repeat the *Pledge of Allegiance*.

I hear words like appreciation, bravery, and honor. No one seems to care that the two returning soldiers don't have the same color skin. I know this is important. No matter what happens or what changes are coming, I feel proud of all the people in our little town.

Finally, Mr. Haley gets up and tells everyone about how many American soldiers have served in Vietnam and how many never returned home to their families. I get a lump in my throat when I hear that. At least, Ted and Mr. Parks made it home. I am so glad that Mom and Mrs. Parks aren't widows. Things sure could be worse. Maybe they will even get better with Ted back home. Perhaps some questions don't need to be answered. We'll see about that.

Finally, we all have Kool-Aid and cookies. It's a good day to spend with friends and family and not think about the future. Why can't good times last longer than a few days or even a few months? When I think some changes will work out for the best, the floor drops out from under my world.

NINETEEN

GRANNY HAS CANCER. I don't understand how medicine called Chemo can make her sicker than before she knew she had cancer. Mom and Ted drive her to Memphis every other week for Chemo treatments. She appears to get weaker and weaker after each trip. Finally, after three months of Chemo, Granny says enough is enough. No more Chemo. Granny has started to lose her hair, and she takes more naps than usual. It's a shock to see Granny's bald head, but she says she doesn't miss her hair, not one bit. She even laughs. "Just think of the money we will be saving on shampoo."

Mrs. Parks brings over several colorful turbans for Granny to try out. She never wears them at home. After a while, she decides she will wear one when she feels strong enough to go to church.

Even though she is too weak to stand and cook, Granny wants to be in the kitchen when Mom is cooking. So, after Fran and I get in from school, get a snack, and finish homework, all four of us end up in the kitchen preparing a meal. Granny sits at the table and peels the potatoes, and then Fran washes them and gets them on the stove to stew. My job is slicing tomatoes, cucumbers, or carrots if we have fresh ones from the garden. Mom always has some beans or peas boiling, and she has learned to make bread almost as good as Granny. Sometimes we have pork chops or bologna with our vegetables, but not every day.

We have some terrific conversations as we work in the kitchen, and Granny always asks about what we learned at school. I report that in science class, we are studying traits that children inherit from their parents. My assignment is to record the color of our parents' and grandparents' eyes, if possible. So, with pad and pencil in hand, I ask mom what color Ted's eyes are. I already know Mom has brown eyes. Granny and Popaw both have green eyes. But Mom never answers me. She almost burns the bologna as she stands in front of the stove, holding the fork but never turning the slices over.

Finally, Granny says, "Turn that burner down, June. We don't want that bologna as hard as a rock. Ruby, Ted will be home soon, and you can ask him yourself about his eye color. Right now, I want you to run out to the garden and see if you can't find us a couple of sweet banana peppers to go with our vegetables tonight. Now, scoot."

When I return with the banana peppers, Granny whispers that I am not to mention eye color to Ted or Mom again. Usually, Granny would bend over backward to help with homework assignments, but not this time.

A week later, Granny is throwing up every day, so she has to spend a week in the Memphis hospital. Since finding eye color seems to be an impossible task, the science teacher gives an alternative assignment for students who don't know their parents' or grandparents' eye color. I could just makeup colors for Ted's parents but decide that's probably not a good idea. I think there are lots of questions in my house with answers that got lost somewhere in the past.

After a few months, both Ted and James Parks get jobs at the sawmill, just fifteen miles outside Franklin. They travel together to save on gas and have become close friends even though they didn't serve together in Vietnam. They happened to be on the same bus heading to Franklin at the time of the crash. James is over six feet tall and never meets a stranger. He loves to tell everyone about his farm and how proud he is to survive Vietnam.

Ted is much quieter and rarely speaks unless someone else tries to bring him into the conversation. He tells us he talks to James sometimes as they travel to and from work, mostly, about his family but never about Vietnam. James says he can tell Ted wants to be a good provider for his family. That is enough for the two men to become friends.

Life in Franklin has settled down almost to normal since the two veterans returned. Sometimes on workdays, our dad drops James off and we have time to catch fish before dark. Granny usually sits on the porch with Mom as Fran, Ted, and I take off to the pond. Sometimes on Saturday, our families get together to cook hotdogs or hamburgers. We always get to stay outside after dark to play while the adults visit on the porch. Good times sure can disappear quickly.

Trouble starts one Friday afternoon when Ted and James have a flat tire on the way home from work. The two men have to walk home and leave the truck on the side of the road. After walking about ten miles, they decide to get a spare tire and return early the next morning.

The following day they find four slashed tires and all the windows broken out of Ted's truck. Someone had painted threats all over the hood — ugly threats about white and black people staying away from each other. They scrawled the "N" word on the seat cover in the cab. The word is all over town before the two men can report all the facts to the Franklin police.

Elvie comes over to tell us the police found footprints all around the truck. He also says the man working at Watkins store is looking at sales records to see who recently bought that color paint. Soon the truck is pulled to the police station and covered with a tarp. The sightseers went home. They will wait to read about any arrests in the *Franklin Times*. Mom tells us if she catches any of us even walking by the police station, she'll ground us for a week.

Elvie seems to know a lot about the investigation, so he is the center of attention at Monday's lunch table. When the lunchroom ladies overhear him mention the paint color and who might have bought it, Principal Dunlap shows up at our table in exactly five minutes.

"Are you students enjoying your lunch today?"

"Yes, Sir," replies every single student at the table.

He knows immediately we are lying since the meatloaf, butter beans, and spinach remain on our trays. So, we all take big bites and put our best principal smiles on. No one has another comment to make.

"I want everyone to remember that no one should be spreading gossip that can cause trouble in our school. Y'all are all good students here, so let's make sure your conversations are about school matters. Do I need to say anything more, Elvie?"

The principal looks at him over his glasses rim. That is his most serious look, and all eyes are on us. I think Elvie will choke on his mouthful of meatloaf before he can swallow and reply. Everyone in the lunchroom is staring at our table. Jesse Adams and some of his friends stand up and look real interested in the whole ordeal. Elvie shakes his head and finally mutters, "No, Sir."

As Principal Dunlap walks around the lunchroom with his hands tucked behind his back, he stops at several tables to exchange principal chitchat with students. When he gets to the table where Jesse Adams and his friends usually eat, he stops and decides to sit awhile. No one dares to turn around and stare, but the noise level in the lunchroom becomes extremely low until Mr. Dunlap finally exits. No one passes in the line while we march up to the window to deposit our empty milk cartons and trays at the kitchen window. We leave quietly, but as soon as the lunchroom door slams, we take off running. Emma, Elvie, Carl, and I go to the far corner of the playground and look around to see if anyone is close enough to hear our words.

"Wow, what is all that about with Principal Dunlap? Elvie, have you been spreading some gossip that is gonna get us all in trouble?"

"No, Carl, I haven't! We have a radio scanner, and I overheard Officer Blue say that they have traced the black paint back to someone in town, but that man seems to have left the country."

"He, who?" I ask.

"I better not call any names because yesterday, mother unplugged the scanner and told me if we weren't careful, our car tires might get slashed too."

"All this talk of police and tires being slashed is new to me, and it makes me nervous. I'm gonna run to the bathroom before the bell rings," says Carl as he runs toward the main building.

Emma and I look at each other.

Then Elvie whispers, "Mother thinks it might have been Frank Adams, Jesse's dad. She was in Watkins store a few days ago, and she overheard Mrs. Adams ask Mr. Watkins what her family owed on their charge account. She thought they would be moving to Austin soon. She even said her husband had already started a new job there."

I think Emma might cry, but instead, she grabs my arm, sticks out her chin, and says, "That is the best news I've heard in a long time!"

TWENTY

OUR LITTLE TOWN OF Franklin seems to be changing. Did it start when the Booker T. Washington students enrolled in an all-white school? Did it start when a bus wreck in Jackson put two Vietnam soldiers in the same hospital? Did it begin when Martin Luther King, Jr. got shot in Memphis, Tennessee? I don't know for sure. But one big change came when my family and Emma's family decided to have a Fourth of July cookout. I can't remember the last time that my mom's been so excited about company coming. Ted says nothing will keep him from enjoying time with his family and friends, especially not fear. He even mentions the fear he had known in Vietnam. He says those days are past.

Ted and Mr. Parks are making plans for horseshoes, tug of war, and even a game of Red Rover. When I mention four kids couldn't play Red Rover, Granny informs me that Elvie, Carl, and two families from our church are coming. Then she says Mayor Jones and his family are invited, too. This will be the best Fourth of July ever. Everyone has a job in getting the fire pit ready for the big hotdog roast, setting up sawhorses and plywood tables, measuring off the distances for the horseshoe pegs, and cleaning up every room in our house, even though we all are staying outside.

Emma spends Friday night with me. We are up early digging in the barn for something long enough to have a Tug of War contest. Granny says Popaw's longest ropes are in a barrel under the loft, so off we go. Fear of spiders and other creepy critters doesn't slow us down for a minute. Thomas and Elvie show up and offer to help us look around the barn, but later they decide to try their hand at throwing horseshoes. I have to bite my tongue when Elvie says that a barn could be a dangerous place for a couple of girls to be all alone. I'm thankful that Ted speaks up and says he will unlatch the door and stay close until we find the ropes. Ted and Mr. Parks often laugh at their two daughters who they say are growing up too fast to suit them.

The afternoon is full of games, laughter, and food. Hotdogs roast on the end of a stick, and watermelon slices and homemade ice cream make the day complete. No one asks questions about the damage to Ted's truck, which still hasn't been repaired. By this time, the sheriff has filled out the reports, impressions have been made of footprints, and paint samples collected. No arrests have been made. The people in town just don't want to talk about the incident. Ted and James Parks are glad to put the whole mess to rest. Today is a good day to enjoy the sun and fun. No one is thinking about flat tires, busted windshields, and that terrible "N" word. Then we hear the sirens. Both fire trucks from the south side of town are headed north. Two teenagers on bikes stop to yell the news.

"The school is on fire!"

Franklin Elementary School is engulfed in flames. Ted and some of the other men take off running. The mayor loads up several of us in his station wagon, and soon over half of the town is standing across the street from the school. By the time the fire engine arrives, only a tiny part of the lunchroom has a roof. The main buildings, which house grades one through twelve, lay in a smoldering heap of rubble. No one has the heart to think about what will happen to the students of Franklin in two months. Summer will be over, and school can't start without these buildings being repaired. Where will all the money come from to make these repairs? Only time will tell what caused the sudden destruction of a school that had stood for more than a hundred years. Although this day is the Fourth of July, there doesn't seem to be anything left to celebrate. Did the fire start from some careless fireworks set off too close to the school? Is this fire the result of an angry school patron who wants no part of an integrated Franklin Public School? Again, too many questions are left unanswered.

Someone has to plan for the education of over four hundred students who will need a place to go to school. Mr. Haley and a group of concerned parents ask to meet with the school board as soon as possible. Ted and James Parks offer their support, too. Soon a plan comes together, a plan that just might work if prejudice doesn't get in the way. If so, the plan will be a first for the state of Mississippi.

"Heaven help us," Granny says when she hears the

unlikely plan.

The School Board of the Franklin Public School plans a meeting in the First Methodist Church on the first Tuesday in August at 7:00. Two weeks before the meeting, five families come to our house for supper. This night isn't a Sunday, but the preacher and his wife come too. Granny and Mom cook while Fran and I clean every corner of our house. Granny says the kids can take their plates out on the front porch so the adults can gather around the kitchen table to talk.

The fire has destroyed a big part of our school grounds. I know that it will take more than fire to change some attitudes about skin color around Franklin. Mr. Haley tells us we must find a way to convince our community that if we all work together to help our children get educated, maybe the hard hearts of the past can be changed. Some hearts, like those of Jesse Adams and his family, are full of hate. Granny will whip my backside if she hears me say that. She says I have a hard heart sometimes. Maybe she is right.

The idea that Ted, James, and Mr. Haley have come up with must be important. The mayor's family is here, and citizens of Franklin pack our kitchen until after 9:00. The kids eat supper on the porch and follow it with a game of Hide and Seek in the dark. We haven't had such fun since the school fire cut short our Fourth of July picnic. Even though Elvie gets stuck hiding under the porch, and Thomas runs straight into the clothesline and quits breathing for a few minutes, we have a glorious time.

Emma just doesn't seem like herself, but she did come

running when Thomas hit that clothesline. Most of the time, she sits on the porch talking to Todd, the mayor's son. He didn't act like he knew Emma or me until after the fire. Since the day Emma and I hand-delivered invitations to supper at our house to the mayor, principal, and school board members, Todd and Elvie walk by my house anytime that Emma and I are on the front swing. I am so glad they have never stopped. They just wave, and Emma even waves sometimes.

The entire town is talking about the big decision they must make soon. Finally, the night arrives, and there is tension in the air. It's been years since this many people have shown any interest in a town meeting. The school board president calls the meeting to order. The mayor stands up first to thank everyone who has made suggestions and asks for patience from everyone as the board announces the plan. The school board president reports Franklin Public School Cafeteria can be repaired with a grant from the Mississippi Education Department. This work will start in a few weeks. Classroom space will be built from an increase in local taxes. A tax increase will have to wait for a school vote next year since the deadline for filing has passed. Students in grades one through six will attend classes at the local churches for the next few years. Buses will take them to the newly repaired cafeteria daily.

Students in grades seven through twelve will be bussed down the road to the Booker T. Washington School as soon as the board can raise funds to repair those buildings. Silence fills the room. Then murmuring starts in the back of the room. The mayor calls for silence.

"Anyone wishing to ask questions, please raise your hand and be recognized before speaking. We welcome all comments and appreciate your interest in coming tonight."

The mayor has the same problem that Mr. Haley has in class once in a while. Some people don't want to raise their hands, but they sure can raise their voices.

"Why can't we just repair the buildings right here in Franklin?" someone asks.

"Gas sure don't come cheap. We don't want our kids to spend that much time on a bus," the hardware store owner calls out.

"Why won't the Mississippi Education Department make a loan so that we can keep our kids in Franklin?" A very expectant mother has tears in her eyes.

"Why should we waste money repairing buildings at the Booker T. Washington School? Let's keep our money at home, right here in Franklin!"

"The wear and tear on our buses will sure cause breakdowns. We can't have students sitting on the side of the road while someone repairs the bus," the local mechanic states.

Finally, the bank president rises. "Franklin will be the laughing stock of the state. Whoever heard of bussing white students to a black school? There must be a better plan."

About five families storm out the door. The talk in the

room is so loud that no one even hears the school board president pound his gavel. Mr. Haley goes to the back door and slams it real hard, and then he yells.

"We must think what is best for our students. The kids have welcomed all of the Booker T. Washington students into our school. It's time we learn a lesson from our children about doing what is right. "

Finally, the board president brings everything to order and asks everyone to listen to the next speaker. The next speaker is James Parks, Thomas and Emma's dad. I know that this is a first. Never before has a Black man stood before a group in Franklin, Mississippi, to give a speech. A Black man has never stood in front of a predominantly White audience in Franklin, Mississippi, period. Ted and Mr. Haley stand on either side of Mr. Parks as each man is introduced. Mr. Haley explains that Ted and Mr. Parks had become friends in Vietnam, and each has children attending Franklin Elementary. He mentions Franklin always supports our men in uniform and how well our town is known for its patriotism. This comment seems to stop the low rumble from the back of the auditorium.

Finally, Ted comes down to sit between Fran and me while James approaches the speaker's stand and opens a folder. Thomas, Emma, and Mrs. Parks look around with nervous glances. I give Emma a "thumbs up," and she smiles a little. Mr. Parks speaks with a loud, resounding voice that makes us sit up a little straighter.

"My family has lived just outside of Franklin for over fifty years. I own forty acres that I got from my daddy who farmed soybeans and cotton. That's what I planted too, until I couldn't make a good living for my family. When I got drafted and sent to Vietnam, I didn't want to leave, but the Army pay was more than I could make here on forty acres. When I heard about the fire at Booker T. Washington School, I wanted to get back home to my family bad. I need to say thank you to everyone in Franklin for accepting all the kids into your school. I know it isn't easy, but change never is easy.

"Now, to the matter at hand. All those years that my daddy and I farmed the land, we had to travel to Austin to buy seeds and supplies just like some of you who farm the land. When I mentioned this to a buddy of mine from Vietnam, he knew the problems we have. He farms eighty acres outside Austin. He and his dad wanted to open a Farm Co-op Store when the war in Vietnam started, and he got drafted. Long story short, now he needs a building for his store. He will give us the money we need to rebuild classroom space for Franklin students at the Booker T. Washington school. All we need to supply is the labor.

After two years, we turn the repaired buildings over to him, and we will have a new Farm Co-op Supply store close to Franklin. He has agreed to hire up to ten people from Franklin as full-time workers. I have his proposal run off with all the needed signatures. Please give it your thoughtful consideration and let Mayor Jones and the board of education know what you think by next week.

The school board president explained that the following

year, the community would vote on raising local taxes, and the state department would give Franklin a matching loan. "I am asking you to support that school tax so we can get our new school built right here in Franklin."

I don't hear questions or murmurings as Thomas, Emma, and I pass out the proposal to the crowd. And yes, Todd has to help too, so he takes half of Emma's papers. She could have managed fine without his help. Elvie offers to help me, but I tell him I can manage just fine. The people leave peacefully, and the meeting ends on a much calmer note than it started. Granny says that Mr. Parks impressed many people. She thinks the farmers will go for this idea. I can't say that I am excited about going to school in a church classroom, but it can work. Maybe everyone will be on their best behavior since the preacher will be close by. Maybe God will be a little closer. Thomas, Todd Jones, and Fran are the only people I know very well that might be riding a bus. Fran and I will not be at the same school for two whole years. This plan is looking better and better.

The mayor asks for other suggestions and volunteers. If the proposal is accepted, fifteen to twenty volunteers will be needed to repair the former Booker T. Washington School. The mayor and the School Board believe the call for volunteers is the only solution since no one can think of another way to provide classrooms for almost four hundred students in grades one through twelve. There is not much time or money to make the plan work. Raising taxes is never popular, but educating kids is necessary, so hopefully the new school tax will pass next fall.

As I walk to Watkins Grocery Store to get sugar, flour, and milk, everyone seems to have a worried face. Well, maybe not everyone. Elvie Clark and his mom have visited over half of the people living in the city limits, and they report some families are willing to wait two years to get a new school in Franklin. Granny believes that enough sensible people will work together to repair classrooms at Booker T. Washington, which is already referred to as Franklin Secondary School. I might agree if only more adults would act sensibly. The farmers in the community also like the idea of having a Farmer's Co-op closer than Austin. Granny always says if you can appeal to a person's pocketbook, you are more likely to get them on your side.

Two weeks pass and only ten volunteers agree to work all day Saturday and a half-day Sunday to provide classrooms for students in grades seven through twelve. Ted and Mr. Parks are already working on a supply list and have made two trips to Austin to work out dimensions for ten classrooms and a general assembly hall. Thomas and Emma come over to our house after school to help make posters to encourage more support for Franklin Secondary School. With markers and poster paper sprawled out on the front porch, Thomas asks a question that seems sensible to me.

"Why does the school board and our mayor think that only people over eighteen can make a good volunteer? I have five friends, and every one of them is as tall as my dad. We want to help build our school. What about girls? My sister,

Emma, can drive a nail straighter than I can."

Sitting on the porch swing, Granny smiles at that idea.

"Good point, Thomas. In my day, we girls always pitched in when we had a barn raising. I have driven many a nail in my time, although gripping a hammer isn't as easy for me as it used to be. Let's walk over to the mayor's office and give him an ear full about how many young people want to volunteer. Ted will let your dad know what time if Mayor Jones is willing to listen. Fran, Ruby, and I will arrange a time for you to gather up your buddies, and we will march right into the mayor's office with another proposal."

When Fran hears her name mentioned, she comes outside to the porch.

"I am not marching over to the mayor's office. I couldn't do any volunteer carpenter work. I'm getting ready to polish my nails, and I don't like to work outside and get my clothes all messy. Now, Granny, the doctor says for you to rest more."

"You listen to me, Missy. If the mayor agrees to let young people work, you and I can handle a two-by-four together. I am sure we can fix a hot meal for the workers, and I'm not in the least concerned about your fingernails. There will be plenty of time to rest after school starts back."

With a big sigh and a not so sincere, "Yes, Ma'am," she slams the screen door behind her.

When Ted gets home, we have a family meeting to discuss our proposal to let Thomas and his friends, boys and girls, help repair the Old Booker T. Washington School.

To my great surprise, even Mom speaks up in her most

determined voice. "I like the idea of the teenagers joining in, but if anyone teaches my girls to drive a nail, it will be me, not Granny." She turns to Granny. "Please, Mom, think about your health and what the doctors say about resting more after your Chemotherapy has ended. The girls and I will start working early before it gets too hot. By midmorning, we will get back home to help with lunch delivery. No more discussion about using senior citizen workers in the hot sun."

The look on Granny's face is something to behold. I suppose it's the first time anyone has called her a senior citizen. She doesn't look happy, but when Ted scoots his chair over and puts his arm around her shoulders, she softens up a little. When he mentions he looks forward to her homemade biscuits every day for lunch, she breaks into a smile.

"Well, I guess that is one thing this senior citizen can do without argument. I can make biscuits to help these kids get back into school by the first of October."

TWENTY-ONE

WITH MAYOR JONES AND the school board's approval, twelve parent volunteers, eight high school students, and a few willing young ladies begin work on August 20. The group only has nine weeks to work, but the Mississippi State Board of Education has agreed to allow Franklin Public School to start later if needed. Fran, Mom, and Ted leave at four o'clock every morning, and Granny and I stay behind to clean up breakfast. I go off to attend school at the Franklin Church of Christ.

Mrs. Clark and others have made generous donations to ensure we have all the textbooks we need. Being bussed to the newly built lunchroom is the highlight of our day. Without the students from the upper grades, lunchtime is much quieter. After eating, we have a fifteen-minute recess before boarding the bus back to the church to finish our school day.

Seeing the new desk brought into the Bible classrooms seems weird. Adjusting to charts about the sixty-six books of the Bible on display in every classroom takes a while. All the students seem to be on their best behavior. Maybe the many posters in the halls of pictures of Jesus and Bible scriptures remind us to love our neighbor. But, after about a month, everyone is back to normal behavior, which can be rather rowdy. The boys start running down the halls to get to the water fountain, and the noise in the lunchroom is back to a roar. Even several spitballs have been launched, so yes, behavior is back to normal. Loving your neighbor seems to be a thing of the past. Church school is much the same as regular school.

Granny has made me promise to come straight home to help prepare supper for the family, who works until dark every day except Sunday. Soon Fran forgets about all her broken fingernails and even starts to brag about the number of nails she can drive without Ted having to pull them out for her to try again. On Fridays, we have an extra bunch of biscuits and sausage, apple pies, and extra gallons of tea to prepare for the lunch on the grounds at the school site on Saturday. I don't mind getting up at 4:00 to load Ted's truck because I get a chance to help in the building.

Now, getting up on Sunday morning to be in Bible class by 9:30 is another story. The threat of staying home on Saturday does a lot to help me open my eyes every Sunday during those warm August mornings. I'll not lie. I do miss my fishing trips and sleeping late on Saturday seems like a thing of the past, but I want to do my part. More people from the town begin to drive out to the Booker T. Washington school site. They want to see what this new Franklin Secondary School will look like, even if it's temporary. Ted says they even pick up about twenty more volunteer parents.

The school is not yet finished even after weeks of volunteers working from dawn to dusk, every Saturday and Sunday afternoon. After harvest, some local farmers come to work daily, so soon the building begins taking shape. Joe Samson, James Park's friend from Vietnam, comes to oversee the work and praise the efforts of the town's volunteers. It sure seems good to see blankets spread on the ground on Saturday while about thirty students and volunteers enjoy Granny's biscuits and sausage. Other treats show up from time to time. Elvie and I get into a habit of making four batches of Mississippi Mud cookies after school. We send them by Fran to pass out during work breaks on the following day.

When Todd Jones finds out what we are doing, he asks Emma to help him make peanut butter cookies to send over every Saturday. Mrs. Jones isn't a bit happy about Todd asking a black girl to help make the cookies. She says that it's just not appropriate for the mayor's son to engage in this kind of activity. Please! Prejudice is prejudice, no matter how you word it. I even tell as much to Todd, but not in front of Emma.

The last Saturday of work on Franklin Secondary School finally arrives. We put a second coat of paint on the walls, varnish the wood floors, and hang blackboards in every classroom. Finally, the school is completed, with all the material donated by the Samson family from Austin. This will be a temporary school for Franklin's students, but Joe Samson and his father come most days with words of encouragement. In the future, this will be the Samson Farmers Co-op, a business much needed in our community.

The entire town is invited to tour the new building on the following Saturday. Todd asks Elvie if he and Emma will help us in baking cookies for the grand opening. Elvie says sure. Does he ask me? NO. Does he ask Granny? NO. When Granny overhears this conversation, what does she say? Granny says her kitchen was always open to anyone doing a good deed to help our Franklin students.

Over one hundred town people, black and white together, gather to see the new building that will provide classrooms for grades seven through twelve. We all listen to the school board, the mayor, and the city council say words of praise and thanks for all the volunteer work. Nice new desks for teachers and students were provided by the Samson family. After refreshments, everyone heads back to town with a feeling of goodwill. How long will this last? We'll have to wait and see.

Soon, we all start into a new routine every school day. Fran has to catch the bus first at 6:45. I ride over to my classroom at the Franklin Church of Christ with Ted, who then drives over to pick up James as they start a construction job at Austin. Mom walks to work several days at the Holt Drug Store. Emma's mom is able to work at the new cafeteria. Every day she packages up lunches to be sent out to the new school building. Fran, Todd, and Thomas are starting ninth grade, so once again, Emma, Elvie, and I are together every day at our church school. Also, Todd becomes Emma's shadow every Saturday. If I want to meet Emma on Saturday at Holt's Drugstore for ice cream, she is busy helping Todd with homework. Sleepovers on Friday night are a thing of the past. When I mention to Elvie that I am getting so tired of Todd always being around, he says I'm just jealous because I'm losing my best friend to the mayor's son.

"Elvie Clark, you take that back, or you're getting my fist on your upper lip!"

When I raise my voice, a few kids on the bus look over at us and start whispering to each other. He just turns around and walks to the back seat of the bus and never says another word.

Emma suddenly notices that Elvie moved, so she scoots over to my seat.

"What's wrong with Elvie? Is he mad or something?" Emma asks.

"You don't care what's wrong with Elvie or me. Just forget about your so-called best friends. I am sure you will see Todd this weekend. Right? He seems to have all the answers you need." Emma drops her head and moves to the back of the bus to talk to Elvie. When the bus finally gets back to school after lunch, I feel like I might just throw up. The preacher ends up taking me home early. I march into the house, go straight to my room, and never say a word to Granny. But Granny has several words to say to me.

"Come outside on the front porch, Ruby. The preacher says we need to talk about what happened on the bus today."

"Now?"

"Yes, now, unless you think you need a dose of Castor Oil

for that upset stomach that's keeping you from doing your schoolwork this afternoon."

"My stomach is much better now. No Castor Oil, please."

Granny and I sit on the porch for a good fifteen minutes, just swinging back and forth, enjoying the quiet of the fall afternoon. More and more leaves are falling from the oak trees that line the drive to the house. Then there is the aroma of all those leaves. Popaw said once it was an earthy smell because things that used to be alive were going through a change. Too much change has come to our little town of Franklin, some good and some bad. Some of those changes are downright rotten

"What are you thinking about, Ruby girl?"

"Stuff changing."

"What kind of stuff would that be?"

"Stuff, like I don't want to talk about."

"Sometimes talking about that stuff makes it seem not so upsetting. Could it be the kind of stuff that could cause a stomachache?"

"I did have a stomachache, ya know? I mean, when I got…upset on the bus, I forgot all about lunch. Hard to believe I forgot about eating."

"I would say you have a lot on your mind if you don't think about missing lunch. I made a batch of oatmeal cookies this morning. Do you want some now?"

"Yes, to the cookies, but I don't want to talk about that other stuff now. I don't have to, do I?"

"No, child, you don't have to talk now. Maybe later. After

cookies and milk, we do have some chores to do. Let's carry some water out to the back trees and flowers."

As we fill the water buckets and start down the slight slope of our backyard, I notice something hanging from the top branch of the tree that Ted planted over ten years ago. The closer we get, I can tell it's a rope, a short rope someone tied in a series of knots with a loop at the end. I stop walking and look closer as I swallow a mouth full of air. I saw a picture of that type of rope hanging from a tree in a social studies book when we studied the Civil Rights Movement and the Klu Klux Klan. I set down my bucket and grab hold of Granny's sleeve.

"Come on, child, if I can make it down this hill, I know you can. What are you staring at, Ruby?"

As Granny puts her bucket on the ground, she turns and looks upward. She adjusts her glasses, then looks around on either side of the land that surrounds our house. I will never forget the look on Granny's face. I have never seen her square her mouth like that, and her eyes are glassy but not with tears. Maybe fear, but fear of what? She grabs my hand and almost drags me back to the house. All of a sudden, she's forgotten those water buckets. As we go up the porch steps, two at a time, I'm sure there is no blood flowing into my hand because of Granny's firm grip. She even takes the time to lock the screen and the wood door behind her. Most of the time, we don't bother to lock the doors at bedtime. Granny looks worried as she locks the front door too, draws all the curtains together, and tells me we have work to do getting supper ready. Then she says, "No talking."

When I decide that enough "no talking" time has passed, I mention that I saw a picture of a rope just like that in my social studies class. The look I get from Granny tells me that enough "no talking" time hasn't passed. She doesn't want to hear anything about that rope. She begins to chop onions with a vengeance, her knife echoing off the wooden cutting board. She tells me to wash and dry the few dishes in the sink, set the supper table, and then get the broom and sweep the living room floor. Adults! Sometimes they want to talk, talk, talk; sometimes, they demand no talking. One thing you can always depend on is they will come up with chores when they want to silence a kid.

Around five o'clock, just as I finish sweeping, Granny informs me supper is ready on the stove. She is going to sweep and mop her bedroom. Fran gets home first and asks me why Granny is scrubbing her bedroom floor. I shrug my shoulders and keep cleaning.

"Is Granny mad or something?"

"I'm not sure, but she is not in a mood to talk, ever since we started to carry water down to the trees in the backyard."

"That makes no sense, Ruby. Did y'all water the trees out in the back or not?"

"No, the buckets are still full of water out there."

Granny comes out of her bedroom carrying her mop and bucket of water just as Mom and Ted walk in the front door. They both seem to be in a good mood until they hear the tone of Granny's voice.

"Fran, you and Ruby get the food set on the table and get the glasses full of water. June, I need you and Ted to help me out in the backyard with the water buckets."

Mom and Ted look as confused as Fran, but when Granny assigns you a chore, you best get to it without taking the time to ask a question. Even Mom and Ted know that bit of information, probably better than Fran and I do. When the back porch screen slams shut, Fran crosses her arms over her chest and wrinkles her brow.

"Ruby, why in the world didn't you help Granny with those water buckets?"

"I tried, really. We got about halfway down there when I spotted something hanging from the top branch of that tree that Ted planted. Someone has been out in our backyard and left a rope up there. It scared Granny. I told her what I knew about the KKK. I said a rope like the one in the tree was used in some hangings. She turned white as a ghost. She grabbed me and forgot those buckets. Granny hasn't been herself since. She locked the doors, pulled the curtains, and has been moving around faster than usual. What do you think she wants Mom and Ted to do?"

"Oh, no. The Klu Klux Klan has been active around here since Granny was a little girl. Once, Mom told me about a hanging in Popaw's family that was in all the papers. Popaw's cousin did the hanging. Promise me you won't ask any more questions. I mean it, Ruby, not another word."

Fran runs back to the front door and locks it. She locks the back door, too. Now, Granny, Mom, and Ted are all locked out of the house. Fran is pacing back and forth in the living room, and supper is getting colder by the minute. This has not been a good day for me. I was hateful to Emma, Granny is not herself, and now to learn our family was involved in a hanging. It's too much. Yes, I am worried, but mostly I'm just hungry.

Before we can sit down to eat supper, the Franklin Police Chief and his deputy show up at our front door. They walk around looking for footprints and even bring along a ladder to take down the rope. The noose is now in a plastic bag, and it reminds me of a snake getting ready to strike. They ask a million questions like how often we go down to the back of our property, who is at home during the day, and what neighbors live in the next house about a mile away. Granny says she hasn't noticed any strangers walking down the road. They leave to talk to the Martin family, our closest neighbors, and finally, at about 8:00, we have supper. I am the only one who seems to have an appetite, and after Ted says a rather long prayer, Granny announced she has got to rest her back. After Granny leaves the table, we finish the rest of the meal in silence.

The following day, Saturday, we don't have to hurry around so much. Before noon, the Police Chief is back along with a stern-looking older man. His hair is slicked back with some shiny black cream, and he looks like his face might crack if he tries to smile. No one has to tell me to stay quiet. He scares me to death.

I gladly go to sit on the front porch when Mom asks Fran

and me to go outside while they all talk in the kitchen. I overhear Ted mention the NAACP. The man with Chief Gann is from Jackson, and I guess he is pretty important, even though he doesn't know how to smile. Fran can't believe that I don't know anything about the NAACP. Why don't people say what they mean? Using all those letters is downright confusing to me. It took almost a year for me to figure out that the FBI is part of the police that work for the United States government. Now, someone is sitting in my house who works for the police that wants to advance colored people. Emma and Thomas will never believe this. What in the world will Elvie say? He won't believe me when I tell him. I think about my friends and hope they aren't upset with me.

That night at supper, Ted tells us not to mention what Granny and I discovered in the backyard. He says fingerprints have been taken, and a police car will drive by our house several times a day until the investigation is over.

The next day after church, Elvie grabs me by the sleeve and says we need to talk. He asks me to meet him that afternoon in front of the post office because he thinks my life is in danger. He has no idea what he is talking about, but at the same time, I am curious. So, about an hour after lunch, I tell Mom I want to walk to the post office to check out the new poster about the county fair. When I arrive, Elvie is sitting on the curb with his chin in his hands. He looks like he's lost his best friend. He wastes no time before he starts asking questions.

"Why was a police car sitting in your driveway yesterday

afternoon for three hours? My mom thinks the sheriff called in a man from the FBI to investigate a murder. Who is the shooter? Did anyone have to go to the hospital? Does all this have anything to do with the fires in Franklin?"

"No one got murdered…at least not lately."

"Now, Ruby, tell me the truth. Did an FBI man come over to your house or not?"

"No, and that is the truth."

"Well, what did you mean no one got murdered lately?"

After a long pause, I decide to keep Elvie in the dark for a while because of a strange feeling I have. Elvie doesn't seem to be angry with me about the conversation on the bus.

"The man who came to talk to my granny is from the NAACP. Remember, Mr. Haley told us about the Civil Rights Movement. That is how I knew that the National Association for the Advancement of Colored People has something to do with prejudice and how African Americans have been mistreated."

"But why would the police bring in someone from the NAACP? Tell me the truth, Ruby, has this got anything to do with the fires we've had lately?"

Before I can think of any more information about the NAACP, Elvie interrupts my concentration and asks if yesterday's visit had anything to do with Ted's truck being trashed last summer. I haven't even stopped to consider that question. Elvie tells me that the sheriff hasn't been able to find where the Adams family is living now. When I can't hold it in any longer, I blurt out all I know about the rope in our backyard. I spill all the mystery of Granny's fear of the KKK, or at least the little bit I know about it. I feel glorious knowing more than Elvie. The look on his face is priceless. Yes, it is worth the lie that I told him about the NAACP. I ask him to promise not to tell anyone, or I will get in big trouble. He promises. I just hope he will be better at keeping secrets than I am. He already has shown to be a better friend than me.

Sunday afternoon is quiet. Granny is still cooking and cleaning like the President himself might be coming to visit. When she retreats to the front porch swing, Mom and Ted go for a walk down at the creek. Fran and I have a minute to talk about the dark secret from Popaw's past and the KKK.

"Please, Fran, tell me what you know about Granny's fear of that rope in our backyard. I will never bring it up to Granny because I saw the fear in her eyes that I hope never to see again. Even Elvie has questions about the police coming here. Knowing the facts just might help keep down the crazy rumors that are bound to get started."

"Ruby, I don't know much about things that happened around here over sixty years ago. Popaw mentioned once that his cousin, James Moore, went to prison for lynching a black man. Yes, his cousin was a Klans member. Popaw and his family had very little to do with that side of the family. But he did say that the black man left behind a family with six kids. The oldest daughter was Granny's best childhood friend. Her name was Josie, and she cleaned the house for Granny's mother. After the trial, Josie's family would have nothing to do with the Moore family. Later, when Granny met and married Popaw, Josie never spoke another word to Granny. That is all I know. I promise. But losing a best friend can be hard, especially when there is so much anger. That noose brought back sad memories from a time when anger and prejudice were normal for many people. Think how you would feel if something happened to Emma's dad and you never got to see her again. Please, let's forget about the past. No more questions."

"Popaw's cousin hung a black man. Wow! I'm glad he went to jail."

One of Mr. Haley's favorite sayings is that we must learn from the past or be doomed to repeat those same mistakes. Yet, forgetting about the past doesn't seem like a good idea to me. Just look at all those years that Ted has been gone. I certainly have more questions than answers from my past. After learning about Granny losing her best friend, a plan starts to nag at my brain. The story of a girl named Josie whose father was killed by James Moore and other members of the KKK has to be recorded in the newspapers, even more than sixty years ago. If only Franklin had a public library, I know I could find out what happened to the family after the lynching of Josie's father. Another trip to the Austin Public Library is out of the question. I learned something from the first secret trip to the library because secrets can eat you alive even if you are very careful. And by now, I've learned lying can sure get ya in heaps of trouble.

Maybe Elvie can gather some information from his mother. Mrs. Clark is a member of the Daughters of the

American Revolution, and her family's ancestors arrived on the Mayflower. At least, that's what Elvie has told every history teacher that would give him a chance to brag. I have heard that story since first grade. Maybe she knows someone still living that might remember about a lynching of a black man in Franklin. Perhaps finding Josie will help Granny smile again.

Elvie was only too glad to talk with his mother about the history of Franklin, mainly because her father served as mayor for three terms. As the only daughter of the mayor, she got to attend special meetings at the state capitol. She had secret hopes of Elvie following in his grandfather's steps. According to Mrs. Clark, the town flourished under the leadership of Horace Ashlock. He built the finest city hall in the entire county, installed water lines all over town, and the miles of electric lines more than doubled during his terms of office. Elvie enjoys the conversation for a while then gathers his courage to ask a question about the activities of the Klu Klux Klan in the area. Mrs. Clark's tone changes suddenly.

"Now, Elvie Eugene, that is not a subject we need to talk about. Why bring up that terrible part of Franklin's past that none of us are proud to remember? Just the mention of those people who burn crosses on someone's front yard gives me terrible chills. Oh, Elvie! How could you bring this up? I feel a terrible migraine coming on now. I must get my medicine, turn off the lights, and go straight to my bed. Don't you dare speak another word to me about the KKK."

As Elvie and I sit on the front porch drinking Kool-Aid

and eating popcorn, we both have wrinkled brows. We are trying to decide on another place to get information about the dark time in Franklin's history. Elvie refuses to say anything else to his mother, which is a good idea. I personally have never even heard of a migraine, but from the look on Mrs. Clark's face, that condition must be painful.

I ask Elvie if he thinks Mr. Haley might help us, but he didn't grow up in this area. We both agree that is another dead end. Elvie thinks about the oldest lady at church. She just celebrated her ninety-fifth birthday at Elvie's house. After setting up ten chairs, he hung around to get some cake. She is almost deaf and very forgetful, too. Elvie says Mrs. Harriet Johnson asked five times who the birthday cake was for, even after opening several presents. For lack of a better idea, we plan a trip to visit Mrs. Harriet Johnson in the Happy Acres Nursing Home. We have to get our story straight and come up with a believable excuse to visit Mrs. Johnson. We will need to do some thinking.

TWENTY-TWO

PREACHER BREWER'S LESSON ON Sunday catches my attention. Well, not the entire sermon, but he mentions that it's every Christian's duty to visit the widows and orphans. As I sit trying my best to concentrate on what pure religion might mean, it dawns on me that widows include Mrs. Harriet Johnson in the Happy Acres Nursing Home. I grab a pencil and paper and start writing a few notes from the lesson, and Granny gives me a thumbs up right here in the middle of the church. After lunch, I announce that Elvie and I would like to visit the Happy Acres Nursing Home next Saturday afternoon.

"Why would you want to do that? Whoever do you know that lives there?" asks Granny.

"Well, no one in particular, but I bet there are people who will enjoy getting some fresh flowers or a visit."

"I think this is a wonderful idea, and it warms my heart to hear you say this. I might go along with you and Elvie. Let me know when you get ready, so we can gather flowers or maybe bake some cookies."

Now I have to make sure the trip to the nursing home will

be while Granny is busy with other Christian duties. When Granny asks again about the nursing home visit, I tell her that Elvie is too busy to go because his mother is sick. There is a little truth in that statement. His mother seems to develop aches and pains pretty often.

Nearly a month later, Granny mentions she needs to visit Mrs. Porter from her Sunday school class next Saturday. Her friend is finally getting out of the hospital. The ladies from the church are taking food to feed the family of six for a week. Without a word to anyone, Elvie and I make our trip to the nursing home that same Saturday that Granny is cooking for the Porter family. We take along some flowers that Elvie picks from his mom's prize-winning rose garden.

As we enter the front door, I realize that Mrs. Harriet Johnson may not be healthy enough to have visitors. But if I can get information about Granny's friend from the past, I am going to try. We see many people in wheelchairs and others walking around without even looking where they are going. We ask at the front desk about Mrs. Johnson. The lady says what a pleasant surprise it is for Mrs. Johnson to have some visitors. She also reminds us to talk loud and slow because the old woman is almost deaf. With our questions in hand, we slowly walk to room 215 in the north wing. Elvie looks at me, and I think he may back out and run to the front door. He seems nervous, just like I feel, but I am determined to find answers about Granny's friend Josie.

Maybe visiting Mrs. Johnson is a mistake, but I hope to have some answers about the history of the Klu Klux Klan in

Franklin, Mississippi. I truly believe you can't learn from the past if you don't know the past. With a gentle knock on the door, we enter the door and meet Mrs. Harriet Johnson. She is in a wheelchair, but as soon as she looks up and sees us, her eyes light up.

"Calvin! Julie! I have been waiting so long to see you two children. Please bend down here and let me give you a hug."

We try to explain that we aren't Calvin and Julie for fifteen minutes, then we give up. When she asks about our parents, we both assure her our parents are doing fine. She loves the flowers and even gets out a few pictures of her children and grandchildren she wants to show us. Finally, in my loudest voice, I blurt out,

"Mrs. Johnson, have you lived your entire life in Franklin?"

"Yes, I have. Born and raised right here on my daddy's farm. Don't you remember visiting the farm and playing in the cotton wagons?"

"What about the Moore family who also farmed around Franklin? Did you know them?"

"Oh, yes, the Moore family was already settled when my Clyde and I moved here from Arkansas. Good farmland. That is why we settled here. Franklin was a good place to raise a family. I had seven children, but the Moore family, they had more kids than we did. There was a whole bunch of those Moore boys. You don't see big families like that anymore." Mrs. Johnson looks right past us and doesn't say a word. We are afraid she may have gone to sleep because she closes her eyes. Then she shakes her head. "Why didn't you children bring your parents along on this visit?"

"Well, they have to work and make a living. Maybe they'll come on our next visit," replies Elvie.

"Well, I am sure glad you two got to come. It gets lonesome here, not getting to see my family. Most of my children left the farm and went off to work in a big city. Do you kids live right here in Franklin?"

"Yes, ma'am, I live in the house with my Granny. Her name is Alice Moore. She was Alice Smith before she married Frank Moore. You said the Moore family also farmed just like your husband did. Did you live close to Frank Moore and his brothers?"

"Hard-working family. That Moore family always managed to have a fine crop. Good neighbors, too. It was hard to believe when one of those boys got into trouble with the law. But we don't need to talk about that. My momma said not to talk about that. You young people must listen to your parents. Don't go getting into trouble. Sometimes people have to go off with the police when they break the law."

"Who broke the law?"

"One of those loud, rowdy Moore boys, but we are not talking about that. Momma said never to talk about that. Sh-sh—no more words about that. Did you say you know Alice Smith? I used to know someone with that name. She had a beautiful daughter and two precious grandbabies. Oh my. Someone did break the law. Can't talk about that—sh-sh."

"Who broke the law? Did someone go to jail?"

"Why no, silly girl. It's God's law....no baby with anyone but your husband. That second little girl had a different father. Sh-sh, let's not talk about that now. Momma would get mad."

Elvie looks at me with a confused expression, and then he stares at the floor. I think hard about what I heard. This lady has memory problems. She even thinks that Elvie and I are her own children. How much can we believe about events that happened over ten years ago, even sixty years ago?

As we sit in silence, the clock beside Mrs. Johnson's bed ticks. I listen to the television with the loud volume in the next room. I didn't notice those noises before. The only sound I am aware of is my heart beating. After a few minutes of silence, I see her eyes are closed, and the nurse enters and whispers something about nap time. We leave the room and go out the entrance door to the sidewalk. All that time, I don't say one word. Finally, I look over at Elvie. He looks as miserable as I feel.

"What do you think Mrs. Johnson means about that second little girl?"

"She is ninety-five years old, Ruby. You can't pay much attention to her memory. Come on. Let's stop by the drugstore and get a soda pop. I'll race ya to the front door to see who orders first."

As he takes off running at full speed, thoughts swirl around in my head. No way can I run. I feel like I might throw up right there on the sidewalk. Mrs. Johnson said she knew Granny. She even said Alice Moore had one daughter and two grandbabies. Did she say that the grandbabies were both girls? Maybe. As I somehow move one foot after another, I wonder if I'm brave enough to tell Granny what I have heard or what I think I heard. I don't want to hear about a baby with a different father. I just wanted to know about someone in the Moore family going to jail. Who says getting to the truth is all that important? I used to think the truth is important, but not so much now. Mr. Haley has told us that we should learn important lessons from the past. What if the truth from the past hurts people you love?

"Come on, slowpoke. I'm starving for a Coke." Elvie stops and looks back. He stands in front of the drugstore, waiting as I look up and almost bump into him. We stand there, eye to eye. Neither one of us knows what to say.

"It's okay, Ruby."

"What's okay? You are not the one who just heard something terrible about your family."

"I don't know anything about my father, and my mother gets a migraine headache every time I bring up the subject. After a while, I quit asking. Doesn't matter anyway. You got your mom, Ted, Fran, and the best Granny in the world. That's more than I've got. Come on, let's get a Coke."

"I won't ever quit asking. It matters to me. I'm going home." I look back as Elvie stands with the drugstore door half-open. His mouth is half-open, too. I walk the long way home as I try to make sense of the scrambled words of Mrs. Johnson. Maybe she doesn't even know Granny's family. Can it be that Fran and I don't have the same father? I thought about the school project when I needed to know something about eye color, and no one at home wanted to mention my family tree. Why? Can this be why Ted left after I was born? Can a different father be a reason my mom went so long without getting out of the house?

Fran is on the front porch. Suddenly, I know I can't look her in the eyes. I stumble going up the porch steps as Granny opens the screen door. I flow right past her, and Fran follows.

"Where in the world have you been all afternoon?" asks Fran.

"That's none of your business."

"Well, excuse me for asking. What is wrong with you anyway? You look like you've lost your best friend."

"I don't have any friends. Don't want any friends either."

I slam my bedroom door. I throw myself onto my bed and start crying so hard I can barely take a breath. I need answers but can't think of a single person to help me. After a while, I hear the door open slowly and feel the mattress sink down as someone sits down and starts to rub my back.

"Do you want to tell me what's wrong?" asks Granny.

"No." My chin is shaking. My nose drips, too. And if things aren't bad enough, I get the hiccups.

"Well, put your head up here on your pillow, and when you get ready to talk, we can have some supper in the kitchen. Remember how much we all love you, Ruby."

As I lay face down on my pillow, I think about all the people who say they love me. Did they just feel sorry for me? No, I have always felt safe and loved and wanted at home. I know my family loves me, but just who exactly is my family? Ruby Ann Kendrick or Ruby Ann Something Else? I feel I am running into a dark place, trying to find myself. The next thing I notice how dark it is outside my bedroom window. As I sit up, I see Fran sitting on the floor at the foot of the bed. The house is quiet, and I can smell a wonderfully sweet smell that makes my stomach growl.

"I'm glad you finally woke up. Elvie has been here for over an hour. He's getting on my nerves. Usually, he talks nonstop, but he is pacing the floor and won't say a word. It's weird."

With a big sigh, I sit up in bed and grab a tissue. Walking slowly to the door, I take a big deep breath. As I put my hand on the doorknob, I turn to look at Fran.

"Thanks for not waking me up. I'm sorry I yelled at you."

"No problem. I've yelled at you a lot. That's what most sisters do, ya know."

As I open the door, there stands Granny, Mom, Ted, and Elvie.

"Come on, everyone, I have just taken sugar cookies out of the oven, and I have poured milk for everyone," says Granny.

Elvie grins and nods. "Thanks, Granny, you only have to ask me once. I'm starving."

With all six of us sitting around the kitchen table enjoying cookies and milk, the questions about what Mrs. Johnson said don't seem so upsetting.

"Elvie told me that y'all went to visit Mrs. Harriet

Johnson this afternoon. Your Popaw and I used to play dominoes with her and her husband. I feel ashamed I have not visited her, but her son told me she has dementia and might not even know me. She's all alone now, which seems so sad. All I have to do is look around this table to be reminded of how lucky I am to be a part of this family," says Granny.

Elvie looks at me and smiles. He raises his glass of milk.

"Here's to the Kendrick family who always makes me feel welcome. You know, my mom has never made a homemade cookie in her life."

Everyone laughs, and I know this is where I belong. Someday all those questions about a different father might be answered. Another day I might learn who put a noose in the tree out in the backyard. Eventually, I may be brave enough to ask Mom or Granny. But not just now. Now I have warm cookies, cold milk, and a family that makes me feel warm inside.

TWENTY-THREE

AFTER BEING ASKED A million times why I am so quiet, I make a decision. I need some advice that I can trust. I know I can't trust Elvie not to tell anyone about our visit to Mrs. Johnson. Whether what she said is true or not, what I heard seems to answer many questions I have had over the past years. But as Mr. Haley often reminds us in doing research, I don't know how reliable the source is.

Are some events better left in the past? If answering these questions means opening up old wounds, is my finding the answers worth all the trouble? This time last year, I would have said I was determined to get to the truth. But finding the truth could turn the world upside down for my entire family. Is finding the truth about why Ted left shortly after my birth all that important?

I need to know, but I'm not so sure about others who have held secrets for so long. Not once has Elvie mentioned the secret that we uncovered by talking with Mrs. Harriet Johnson. Granny is getting weaker and doesn't get out as often. After mom insisted, she visited her cancer doctor, and he told her that indeed the deadly disease had returned. I finally decide to talk to Mr. Haley. Finding a chance to talk without everyone getting suspicious doesn't prove to be difficult. Every other week, Mom takes off work to take Granny to her treatments. No one except Fran is at home until after five o'clock on those days. As much as I hate to include her in this quest, there is no other way. My days of covering up with a ton of lies are over.

When Fran gets home from school on Monday, I know what I need to do. Mom has left instructions about peeling potatoes, slicing up cabbage, and getting the purple hull peas to boiling. Fran thinks she is the only one who knows how to season the peas just right. I have the peas boiling and already seasoned, and I'm chopping the cabbage when Fran finishes her homework. While we peel the potatoes at the kitchen table, I tell her about the trip to the nursing home. She sits quietly listening to my story about Mrs. Harriet Johnson, but when I mention that Mrs. Johnson said Joyce and Frank Moore's granddaughters had different fathers, she slams her hand on the kitchen table.

"Not another word, Ruby. Stop. Granny's cancer has returned, Mom and Dad are finally back together, and you still want to stir up trouble. Quit thinking about yourself and consider what you are saying. There is no good to be done by answering all these questions about the past. Forget all this nonsense."

"Well, it wasn't nonsense when you decided you wanted to take a bus trip to the Austin Public Library."

"That was different, and you know it. That was only to

find out who Granny had been getting letters from. That had nothing to do with Mom and Dad."

There is a strange silence in the kitchen. Fran and I stop and stare at each other. We, or at least I, think about those years when Mom was so different, so not like herself. That change may have started when I was an infant but seems to have gotten so much better since Ted has returned from Vietnam. Maybe the memories of Mrs. Johnson make more sense than either Fran or I imagine. Maybe the truth isn't as important as I had thought. Why should I open wounds that his coming home already healed? Granny always says people can change for the good if the conditions are right. Mom has changed since Ted came home. Our house is more like a home with Ted and Mom together. What right do I have to bring up the past that can make the conditions go in the wrong direction?

"Ruby, don't do anything weird that will upset Granny. If you want to find out about any truth to your suspicions, talk to Mom and Dad. Promise me that you won't call for a family meeting. There is no telling what this kind of talk will do to Granny. Promise me."

"Okay, I promise Granny will never know about what Mrs. Johnson said, truth or lie."

"Thanks, Ruby. Now let's get supper on the table."

Without another word, supper is on the table when the family returns from the doctor. The conversation includes a good report from the cancer doctor. Granny doesn't need more Chemo. The doctor recommended only an additional medication. Granny says she wouldn't take another pill, and Mom rolls her eyes. We all know that this decision will require more conversation later.

"I am so proud of these two young ladies for having a home-cooked meal ready. If I never have to eat another hamburger in my life, I will die a happy woman," Granny says.

"Can we please have no more talk of anyone dying?" says Ted, as he puts his arm around Granny and pats her shoulder.

"Fine with me," said Granny, "but one thing for sure, I am looking forward to more cabbage, peas, and potatoes."

For the next few weeks, I avoid talking to Fran. I tell Granny that Elvie and I have to meet with Mr. Haley after school to work on a special report. I am going over in my head what I should say about the conversation with Mrs. Johnson. I won't include Elvie in this meeting. I'm not even sure I want to have this talk. I trust Mr. Haley, and I desperately need someone to talk about the nagging thought of Fran and me being half-sisters. On Tuesday afternoon, I find Mr. Haley surrounded by piles of ungraded papers.

I ease into the room without a sound. Gathering all my courage, I choose my words carefully.

"I hope you're not too busy to talk for a few minutes." I don't look up. "I have a few questions."

"Never too busy for you, Ruby. Where is that big smile I usually see on your face?"

"Don't have much to smile about these days. I'm just gonna start right into what is on my mind. You are a good listener, and I promise to try to listen to any advice. So many people seem to be affected by my finding out answers that I…if you are too busy.…"

"Slow down, Ruby, and look at me. Take a big breath. Come sit over here. Now tell me, what's got you so worried?"

"I really need to find out who my father is, and I can't decide how to go about asking without upsetting my whole family. You're the only one that seems to know about how to get answers, so what do you think?"

Mr. Haley puts his finger under my chin and looks me squarely in the eyes. My heart is beating so fast. I know my face is as red as the beets Granny raises in her garden.

"Well, that question shouldn't be too hard to answer if we can look at your birth certificate. Why don't you just ask your mom to let you look at it? You are a very inquisitive young lady. I'm sure we can put our heads together and think of a good reason to see the names of your parents that were listed when you were born. Let's not get into a big hurry, but come back after school next Tuesday, and we can talk some more. Does that sound like an answer that might bring back that beautiful smile of yours?"

"Does everybody have a birth certificate?"

"Oh, yes, Ruby, you have a birth certificate. This school needed to see that certificate before you started school. I can see why you wouldn't want to ask your mom the question about who your father is, but for sure, she listed the father when you were born. I will need to give this question some more thought, but don't you worry anymore. A birth certificate is a legal document, and I am sure that your parents recorded it accurately when you were born. Trust me on this, Ruby. You don't need to get upset about this. Okay?"

"Okay, if you are sure about this birth certificate, I do feel some better. Thanks, Mr. Haley. See ya next Tuesday after school. Not a word to anyone about this, cross your heart and hope to die? Well, don't hope to die, but this is important to me."

"I can see how important this is to you. Just remember, some adults will help you with these tough questions. I feel honored that you came to me. See ya next Tuesday. If ya can't find me next Tuesday, just look behind the huge piles of ungraded papers."

I smile as I leave the school building and go straight home to see how Granny is feeling. She seems stronger and even tells Fran and me to stay out of her kitchen until she asks for help cooking. That is good news to me. After a big breakfast of pancakes and bacon on Saturday morning, I decide to find my fishing pole and head down to the pond. Granny says she will help me with the worms for bait. She watches as I pick up two big rocks and find several big nightcrawlers for bait. She looks pleased just sitting down on the ground and handing me a worm when I lose my bait. She even laughs out loud when a small catfish jumps off my line about a foot from the bank. In less than an hour, I am out of bait. Granny lays her head back on the tree where she is sitting and takes a nap. The sun feels so warm. I decide not to wake her. I try my hand at throwing rocks across the pond.

Soon she opens her eyes, stretches her arms up to the sky, and asks me how many fish I caught. I laugh and tell her I threw them back because I don't want to mess with the cleaning.

"Gracious Ruby, you sound just like your Popaw. He used to tell me that same thing whenever he came back empty-handed. I suspect he might have taken himself a long nap, like the one I had. Come here and sit beside me awhile, and let's enjoy this wonderful day the Lord has made."

It isn't long before we hear Mom, Ted, and Fran leaving the house and tromping through the tall grass, making their way to the pond. Mom is laughing at something.

"I told ya I am right. On a sunny Saturday morning, I just knew we would find you two down by the pond," Fran said.

"I simply can't believe y'all came fishing, leaving all of those dirty dishes still in the sink."

"Now, June, those dirty dishes will wait for a while. Let's let Granny and the girls enjoy themselves while we run into town and get some fertilizer for our trees and flowers. Sound like a good plan, Granny? Oh, should we stop and bring in some hamburgers and fries for lunch?" Ted asked.

"I am going to pass on hamburgers and fries, not sure about these girls. I'm planning to bake a fresh peach cobbler, fried bologna, and creamed potatoes will be my lunch. I already got the peaches thawing, but you young people can throw away your money on hamburgers if that is what you want."

"Fried bologna sounds good to me, and peach cobbler

sounds even better," replied Fran.

"I'm eating with Granny and Fran," I answer quickly.

"All right, suit yourselves. We are off to town for a bit." Ted tweaks me on the ear. "I thought maybe we'd have fried catfish for supper, but it looks like the fish aren't biting this morning."

With a sparkle in her eyes, Granny tells Ted and Mom we threw all the fish back. Fran laughs out loud, shakes her head, and sits down beside Granny and me. As I watch Ted and Mom walk back up to the house, hand in hand, just for a moment, I remember my meeting with Mr. Haley on Tuesday after school. Did it matter what names had been recorded on a piece of paper ten years ago? Well, maybe not, but I still need to know. Soon Granny, Fran, and I head to the house, but Granny wants to walk out back and check on the tree growing out by the Crepe Myrtles. Fran and I walk along, too. She hasn't checked on it for months, and she promises we will only stay a minute. When she sees the tree has grown well above her head and is branching out in all directions, she smiles and hugs Fran and me so tight.

"This tree is strong, just like our family is strong now. There will be storms and strong winds, but soon I will be taking my naps under this tree if the good Lord blesses me with good health. Come on, girls. I need to get started on cleaning up that kitchen. I mean, we need to get started."

"Don't forget about the peach cobbler," said Fran.

The next day, after Sunday dinner, Mom announces that she wants to call a family meeting. This is definitely a first for

Mom, but Ted is the one who talked first.

"Yesterday, June and I stopped by the bank to pick up some documents stored in our safe deposit box. Granny mentioned a life insurance policy that she wanted to check on. Seems your grandfather had taken out the policy when you girls were born. So, we have the policy here, and we also have the birth certificates for both of you girls. Granny will make the next announcements."

I can't believe what I am hearing. A life insurance policy for Fran and me? Popaw took out the life insurance policies when he'd had enough money to put some back for his granddaughters? I am so deep in thought that I don't even hear Granny ask me a question until she comes over and puts both her hands on my shoulders.

"Your Popaw loved you girls and wanted to give you a little head start on an education someday. I know Ruby is still in grade school, but soon Fran will be old enough to think about some job training, so your mom and I decided to let you know now about what your Popaw bought for you while you were still in diapers. Well, Ruby, what do you have to say?"

"Why do we need a birth certificate now?"

"We won't need to show our birth certificates until we are ready to get the money. Isn't that right, Mom?" asked Fran.

"Sure, we just want to make sure you girls know about the insurance money. We will need to get the birth certificates back to the bank soon," she replies.

"Would it be alright if I look at my birth certificate before it goes back to the bank?"

"Sure, Ruby. What about you, Fran? Want to look over this to make sure your name is spelled right?" laughs Granny.

As we both pick up the certificates, Fran looks at me and smiles. She seems as nervous as I am while she looks over each line without saying a word. The only line that matters to me is the one that says father. That line reads Ted Kendrick. I finish looking it over, hand it back to Mom, and then hug Granny. And yes, I hug Ted too.

On Tuesday of the next week, I walked into Mr. Haley's room with a big smile on my face. He never looks up from his work until I say, "Thanks so much, Mr. Haley."

"Oh, Ruby, so good to see ya. Thanks for what?"

"Well, I guess, just thanks for always being here."

"That's what friends are for."

"Hey, there is someone out in the hall who wants to come in. That is if you aren't too busy?"

"Sure, tell them to come on in."

"Come on in, Elvie. Mr. Haley said he would be glad to help you find out about your birth certificate."

The End

(Actually, the beginning of another quest for the truth)

www.ingramcontent.com/pod-product-compliance
Lightning Source LLC
Chambersburg PA
CBHW061228170626
46809CB00007B/2569